W9-CHY-010

# FATAL FIRST EDITION

## Titles by Jenn McKinlay

### Library Lover's Mysteries

BOOKS CAN BE DECEIVING
DUE OR DIE
BOOK, LINE, AND SINKER
READ IT AND WEEP
ON BORROWED TIME
A LIKELY STORY
BETTER LATE THAN NEVER

DEATH IN THE STACKS
HITTING THE BOOKS
WORD TO THE WISE
ONE FOR THE BOOKS
KILLER RESEARCH
THE PLOT AND THE PENDULUM
FATAL FIRST EDITION

### Cupcake Bakery Mysteries

SPRINKLE WITH MURDER
BUTTERCREAM BUMP OFF
DEATH BY THE DOZEN
RED VELVET REVENGE
GOING, GOING, GANACHE
SUGAR AND ICED
DARK CHOCOLATE DEMISE
VANILLA BEANED

CARAMEL CRUSH
WEDDING CAKE CRUMBLE
DYING FOR DEVIL'S FOOD
PUMPKIN SPICE PERIL
FOR BATTER OR WORSE
STRAWBERRIED ALIVE
SUGAR PLUM POISONED

### Hat Shop Mysteries

CLOCHE AND DAGGER
DEATH OF A MAD HATTER
AT THE DROP OF A HAT
COPY CAP MURDER

ASSAULT AND BERET
BURIED TO THE BRIM
FATAL FASCINATOR

### Bluff Point Romances

ABOUT A DOG
BARKING UP THE WRONG TREE
EVERY DOG HAS HIS DAY

### Happily Ever After Romances

THE GOOD ONES
THE CHRISTMAS KEEPER

### Stand-alone Novels

PARIS IS ALWAYS A GOOD IDEA
WAIT FOR IT
SUMMER READING

# FATAL FIRST EDITION

## Jenn McKinlay

BERKLEY PRIME CRIME
*New York*

BERKLEY PRIME CRIME
Published by Berkley
An imprint of Penguin Random House LLC
penguinrandomhouse.com

Library of Congress Cataloging-in-Publication Data

Names: McKinlay, Jenn, author.
Title: Fatal first edition / Jenn McKinlay.
Description: New York: Berkley Prime Crime, 2024. |
Series: A Library Lover's mystery
Identifiers: LCCN 2023031299 (print) | LCCN 2023031300 (ebook) |
ISBN 9780593639337 (hardcover) | ISBN 9780593639351 (ebook)
Subjects: LCSH: Norris, Lindsey (Fictitious character)—Fiction. |
Library directors—Fiction. | Libraries—Fiction. | Books and reading—Fiction. |
Murder—Fiction. | LCGFT: Cozy mysteries. | Novels.
Classification: LCC PS3612.A948 F38 2024 (print) |
LCC PS3612.A948 (ebook) | DDC 813/.6—dc23/eng/20230717
LC record available at https://lccn.loc.gov/2023031299
LC ebook record available at https://lccn.loc.gov/2023031300

Printed in the United States of America
1st Printing

Book design by Laura K. Corless

This is a work of fiction. Names, characters, places, and incidents
either are the product of the author's imagination or are used fictitiously,
and any resemblance to actual persons, living or dead, business
establishments, events, or locales is entirely coincidental.

PUBLISHER'S NOTE: The recipes contained in this book are to be
followed exactly as written. The publisher is not responsible for your specific
health or allergy needs that may require medical supervision. The publisher is
not responsible for any adverse reactions to the recipes contained in this book.

*For my father-in-law, Robert C. Orf. You're truly one of the kindest, calmest and least judgmental people I have ever met. You're always there when we need you, and your words of wisdom and eternal optimism are much appreciated. Thanks for being you, Dad. You're the best.*

FATAL FIRST EDITION

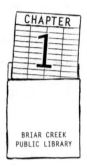

CHAPTER

1

BRIAR CREEK
PUBLIC LIBRARY

H ow's the windy city?" Nancy Peyton asked.

Lindsey Norris glanced at the tiny faces of her friends on her phone. She was missing their weekly crafternoon meeting at the Briar Creek Public Library, where she was the director, and the group had just video called her to see how her archivist conference was going. They were all crammed together, peering into one phone.

"Windy is a very accurate description," she said. She was sitting in a conference room in a sectioned ballroom of the Chicago hotel where the Annual Archivists Convention was being held.

"Who plans a conference in January in Chicago?" Beth Barker asked. She was the children's librarian, and Lindsey could just make out the astronaut costume she was wearing, bubble helmet and all.

"Archivists choose to meet in the off-season so they can spend their money on rare books instead of conferences," Lindsey answered. "I assume outer space is the theme for story time this week?"

"You know it," Beth said. "On the story countdown, we've got *Mousetronaut*, by astronaut Mark Kelly; *On the Launch Pad*, by Michael Dahl; and *Moon's First Friends*, by Susanna Leonard Hill. It's going to be far-out."

The crafternooners behind her collectively groaned, and Lindsey laughed. Beth had been her roommate in library school, and her enthusiasm for children and reading hadn't waned one bit over the years.

"Where's that brother of mine?" Mary Murphy asked. She was squinting into the phone on their end.

"He's braving the mob at the coffee shop in the lobby," Lindsey said. Mike Sullivan, known to everyone in Briar Creek as Sully, was Mary's brother, but more importantly, to Lindsey at any rate, he was Lindsey's husband.

"Good man," Violet La Rue observed. She was a retired Broadway actress who now ran the local community theater and had been a crafternooner with her best friend Nancy Peyton since Lindsey had started the program several years before.

"Did I hear Violet talking about me?" Sully appeared, carrying two cups of coffee as he took the seat beside Lindsey.

Lindsey turned the phone so that their friends could see him. They all cried, "Hi, Sully!" and he toasted them with his coffee cup.

"What's the craft today?" Lindsey asked. Not being the crafty sort, this was the only part of the program that she didn't love, so she wasn't that upset about missing it, but she didn't want to be rude.

"We're working on coiled wire bookmarks," Paula Turner said. She held up a sample of her work in progress. It was the silhouette of a cat with a spiral for a belly. She deftly placed it on a page in the book of the week, which was *A Gentleman in Moscow*, by Amor Towles, and closed the book. It appeared as if the cat was sitting on top of the novel. It looked adorable but also complicated.

"That's amazing!" Lindsey wondered if her lack of enthusiasm was obvious.

"Right, I'll make one for you," Paula said. "I can try and make it look like your cat Zelda."

Lindsey grinned. It was clear she hadn't fooled Paula a bit.

"Not to give you a case of FOMO, but you're missing Violet's pulled pork sliders," Mary said. She held one up to the camera. It looked delicious on its fluffy bun, dripping with barbecue sauce and packed with shredded pork and coleslaw. Lindsey felt her stomach growl.

"Don't be a tease, Sis," Sully said. He grinned and added, "We're going to Monteverde for dinner tonight."

"Now who's the tease?" Mary chided him. "You know it's cruel to taunt a woman who owns a restaurant with the news that you are dining at one of the finest Italian restaurants in Chicago."

"Sorry not sorry," Sully said. Mary shook her head at him.

A man stepped onto the stage at the front of the room and Lindsey said, "We'd better go. The program is about to start. We leave on the train tomorrow, so we'll be home the day after!"

The crafternooners said good-bye and waved. Lindsey ended the call.

"Homesick?" Sully asked as he handed Lindsey her coffee.

"No . . . maybe just a little," she said.

"You're turning into a regular Creeker," he said. He looked pleased as he draped his arm around the back of her chair.

Creekers were what they called lifelong residents of their hometown, Briar Creek. Sully and his sister, Mary, had been raised on the Thumb Islands, an archipelago in the bay off the shoreline village in Connecticut. Lindsey had lived there for only a few years, but the quaint village had definitely become home sweet home to her.

Lindsey's friend Beth took the position of children's librarian in Briar Creek right after they graduated and had encouraged her to apply for the director's position when Lindsey lost her archivist job at the university in New Haven due to downsizing. It had taken some time and a lot of patience to get the small community to accept her. Marrying Sully, a native, had certainly helped.

"That might be one of the nicest things you've ever said to me," she whispered to him.

He smiled at her, and she marveled for the thousandth time that this man, with his reddish brown wavy hair and bright blue eyes, was her husband. They weren't a natural fit. He was a boat captain who ran tour boats and a water taxi in the bay around the islands, while she was petrified of water over her head, especially if she couldn't see the bottom. He was in his glory being outside all day battling the elements, whereas, other than walking their dog Heathcliff or bicycling to work and home, Lindsey preferred to be inside with a book. Still, somehow they clicked, and Lindsey couldn't imagine spending her life with anyone else.

"Good afternoon, everyone." The man on the stage spoke into the mic.

Lindsey recognized him right away. He was Henry Standish, the director of the archivist conference. Because her initial interest in a career in information science had been in preservation, Lindsey had known of him while in graduate school, as Henry Standish had been the curator of a very exclusive private collection on the Upper East Side of Manhattan.

Shockingly, a few years ago, he'd been let go from his elite post amid rumors of fraud. It had been quite the scandal in academic circles, but nothing was ever proven. The taint of the accusation remained, however, ending Standish's curatorial career. Somehow, Standish had landed the coveted position of conference director for the archivist society and had been in charge of the annual meeting ever since.

Lindsey hadn't attended the conference in ages, but having just acquired a rare collection of first editions when a former resident of Briar Creek donated them to the public library, she had felt the need to get back in the game. Sully had been more than happy to join her and had spent most of his time looking up his old Navy buddies in the Chicago area while she sat in on panel discussions about preserving the past.

"I am thrilled to present one of the best book restoration specialists in the country," Henry continued. "She's certified in book arts, conservation and authentication. She's internationally acclaimed and has won the Grand Prize in the Lawton-McNamara Contest. Also, she's come all the way from San Francisco to speak with us, so please give a warm welcome to Brooklyn Wainwright." Henry held out his arm, gesturing to the left side of the stage. The packed room applauded as a pretty blonde on the tall side of medium climbed up the short staircase, leaving a ruggedly handsome, dark-haired man in a bespoke sports coat standing at the base of the steps.

Brooklyn waved as she crossed to the podium, carrying what appeared to be an archival box. She shook Henry's hand and moved to stand in front of the microphone.

"Hi," she greeted the room. The microphone screeched, and she winced and moved back. She cast an exasperated glance over her shoulder at the handsome man, who lifted one eyebrow at her and smiled. When she turned back to the room, she, too, was smiling. "Now that I've got your attention, let's talk book restoration."

Lindsey settled back in her seat. This had been in her top three talks to attend. Brooklyn Wainwright not only was an expert respected in the field but had also been tied to several high-profile murder investigations, which made Lindsey feel that Brooklyn was a kindred spirit, since Lindsey's own life in recent years had also been rife with dead bodies, which was not something a book restorer or a librarian typically dealt with.

Brooklyn was wearing white cotton gloves and holding up a book she had recently restored as an illustration of one that she had returned to its former glory. It was riveting, at least to Lindsey. Whoever was behind her was not nearly as interested. First they rammed the back of her chair. She shifted in her seat and refocused her attention on the stage. Then the person muttered and banged into Lindsey's chair again. She cast a glance at Sully, and he began to turn around, looking as if he was going to say something.

Lindsey put her hand on his arm. He glanced at her, and she shook her head. She didn't want to risk causing a scene during the talk. He sighed and turned back to the stage. Whoever was behind Lindsey knocked her chair one more time, and then she heard them stand up and leave. They actually left! Brooklyn was just getting to the best part, about how she put the books back together once she'd restored them. Well, it was that person's loss.

The lecture ended to enthusiastic applause, and Brooklyn stepped back from the podium. She put the book back in its archival box and stripped off her gloves. The man who'd been standing by the stage watching her now joined her and took the box out of her hands.

Lindsey turned to Sully. "Wasn't that fascinating?"

He raised his eyebrows and said, "I had no idea that a

book from 1840 would be easier to mend than a book from 1940 because the quality of the paper was so much better before they started using wood pulp. She's a very interesting speaker."

"I thought so, too," Lindsey gushed. "I'd love to meet her, but I don't want to be a pest."

Lindsey reached down to grab her shoulder bag from where she'd tucked it under her seat and found the handles of a canvas conference tote bag instead. Her bag! She leaned forward and peered between her legs, pushing aside the long hank of curly blond hair that blocked her line of sight. Relieved, she spotted her shoulder bag under the conference tote that was given to everyone in attendance. She frowned. She was certain she'd left her tote bag in her hotel room. Who did this one belong to then?

She grabbed both bags and sat up. She opened her shoulder bag to check that all of her personal belongings were inside. They were. *Phew.* Then she examined the tote bag. It was beige canvas with the conference logo of an open book printed on the front in a bold shade of blue. The zippered front pocket was empty, but there was an item in the main compartment of the bag. Lindsey glanced behind her to see if whoever was sitting behind her had accidentally pushed their bag under her chair.

The seats were empty; in fact, the entire row was vacant. She wondered if the person who had knocked into her seat had dropped their bag. She glanced around the room to see if anyone appeared to be distressed. The remaining people in the room were chatting and laughing. Hmm. She unzipped the tote and looked inside to see if she could find something to identify the owner.

The only item was a book. Not an extraordinary find, given that she was at an archivist conference that dealt primarily with books and other primary source materials. Lindsey took it out of the bag and examined it. It was a copy of Patricia Highsmith's *Strangers on a Train*. The dust jacket looked vintage with dark colors and haunting portraits of an anguished-looking man and woman. The paper felt fragile, so she carefully opened the book.

"Did you buy a book?" Sully asked.

"No," Lindsey said. "I found it under my seat."

Sully glanced at the chairs surrounding them and then at the people lingering in the room, just as Lindsey had.

Lindsey carefully opened it to the title page. It took her a moment to decipher the handwriting. Then she gasped. "I think this is signed from Patricia Highsmith to Alfred Hitchcock."

"Really?" Sully leaned closer to see. He studied the inscription and said, "I think you're right."

Lindsey glanced back at the spidery writing. It read:

*For Hitch, It was a pleasure. Warmly, Pat*

"If it's genuine, this book has to be worth a fortune," Lindsey said. She pulled out her cell phone and took a picture of the cover and the inscription. The crafternooners would love this! She closed the book and put it back in the bag. "I'm going to ask the speaker what she thinks."

She glanced up at the stage, where Brooklyn Wainwright was talking with Henry Standish while her handsome companion looked on.

"Good idea. Maybe someone brought it to show her and forgot it," Sully said. "Although, that seems highly unlikely."

They rose from their seats and made their way to the dais. The room had thinned out as the panel attendees scattered, hurrying to the next talk on their schedules.

Lindsey tried not to be nervous as she approached the famed book restorer. She'd read articles about Brooklyn Wainwright and watched online videos where she discussed her various projects. She was everything Lindsey had hoped to be when she'd been in library school, studying to be an archivist.

"Excuse me, Ms. Wainwright," she said.

Brooklyn turned away from Standish and gave Lindsey her full attention. "Hi, how can I help you?"

"I'm sorry to bother you, but I have a book here that I was hoping you'd take a look at?" Lindsey used upspeak, turning it into a question so that she didn't sound demanding. She held out the bag and the man beside Brooklyn took it before Brooklyn could.

"Really, Derek?" Brooklyn asked the man, but he ignored her and opened the bag, peeking inside.

"Yes, really, darling," he said. Lindsey noted his British accent and immediately warmed to him as he reminded her of their friend Robbie Vine, also a Brit, back home in Briar Creek. "If I've learned one thing whilst being married to you, it's that books can kill."

Sully turned to Lindsey with his eyebrows raised. "He's not wrong."

Lindsey glanced at Brooklyn, and in that moment, she knew she'd been right, and they really were kindred spirits. Not just in their love of old books but also in the overprotective men they'd married.

"It's clear." Derek handed the bag to Brooklyn.

"Thank you," she said. She took the book out of the bag, holding it gently just as Lindsey had.

She examined every bit of it, cloth cover, edges and spine, and when she opened it and read the inscription, she gasped. "This could be worth a fortune. It's a first edition with what appears to be the original dust jacket, and it's in amazing shape. It'd easily go for several thousand, but the inscription, if authenticated, makes it an extremely rare collectible for fans of both Highsmith and Hitchcock. The bidding war at an auction for this book could be off the charts."

Henry Standish, who'd been speaking with one of the conference volunteers, identifiable by the lanyard and badge that he wore, joined them. "Thank you again, Brooklyn, always a pleasure. Our next speaker is here, however, so . . ."

He made a shooing motion with his hands. Well, that was abrupt.

Brooklyn and Derek exchanged an amused glance. She put the book back in the bag and handed it to Lindsey. "It appears to be in excellent condition. You have quite a treasure there."

"It's not mine," Lindsey said. "I found it under my seat." Henry glanced between them, clearly impatient for them to depart. Lindsey held the tote bag out to him. "Do you have a lost and found for the conference?"

"Yes, of course. You can check with the registration staff," he said. "I'm sure they have one set up right there by the main doors."

He began to walk, ushering them like a flock of ducks across a busy road.

"I've only taken a quick glance at the book, and I'd need more time to be certain, but I think that book is very valuable, as in tens of thousands of dollars," Brooklyn said. "Potentially even more than that."

Henry stopped ushering. He stared at Brooklyn. She had his full attention now. "Excuse me?"

Brooklyn nodded. "First edition, excellent condition and inscribed by the author to a famous movie director? We're talking big money."

"And probably a murder," Derek muttered under his breath. "In fact, I think we need to go so you don't get involved in yet another life-threatening situation."

"Me?" Brooklyn put her hand on her chest, the picture of innocence.

"Sound advice," Sully said. He and Derek exchanged a look of complete understanding. "We should go, too."

"But the book," Lindsey and Brooklyn protested together.

"Will be just fine in my keeping," Henry said. He took the tote bag and peeked inside. He stared at the item, not touching it. Lindsey thought he went a little pale, but that could have been the overhead fluorescent lighting. Abruptly, Henry shook his head and lifted the bag in the air. "Penny!"

"Yes, Mr. Standish?" A young woman with dark brown hair pinned into a donut-shaped bun at the nape of her neck and wearing thick-framed black glasses hurried across the stage toward them. She had on a headset and was carrying a clipboard. Judging by the dark circles under her eyes, she hadn't slept in days.

"Take this!" Henry held out the bag to her. Both Lindsey and Brooklyn cried out, protesting the rough treatment. Henry glanced at them and said, "My assistant, Penny Minton, will take care of it." Then he turned back to Penny and said, "This item is of particular interest." He met and held Penny's gaze. Lindsey felt as if there was an unspoken conversation happening there, and he added, "Be careful with it. It's potentially very valuable."

"Yes, sir," Penny said. She took the bag, cradling it close. "Um . . . what is it?"

"A book, obviously," Henry snapped. "It was left in here during the last program. I haven't got time to deal with lost and found items, so you'll have to find whoever lost it and return it to them." Again, he met and held her gaze. She gave him a small nod.

"Of course, Mr. Standish," Penny said. Her eyes were wide behind her glasses as if she had no idea how she was going to accomplish such a thing.

"I could take . . ." Lindsey and Brooklyn said at the same time while both Sully and Derek shook their heads.

"No need," Henry said. "I've got this. Don't fret, ladies, I am a professional archivist, after all."

Brooklyn frowned, and Lindsey knew she was doing the same. The entire situation felt very unsatisfactory.

"Henry!" An older woman strode across the stage toward them. "I need water with a slice of lemon in it, no ice and a mic check. I'm on in five!"

"Yes, Adriana, right away. You heard her." Henry nudged Penny with an elbow, and she hurried forward with the book bag clutched beneath her clipboard. "Step lively, Penny, and try not to bungle things this time."

A flurry of people appeared wielding makeup brushes and hair spray—apparently Adriana came with an entourage—separating Lindsey and Sully from Brooklyn and Derek. Lindsey waved, and Brooklyn smiled and waved back before she was swallowed up by the next speaker's crew.

"It's too bad there's another speaker scheduled in this room. I would have liked to talk to Brooklyn some more," Lindsey said.

"She and her husband, Derek, definitely felt like our people, maybe we'll see them again," Sully said. "Come on. According to your schedule, we're to be in conference room H for a discussion on web archiving."

"Right," Lindsey said. "I don't want to miss that. So much stuff published online is ephemeral in nature, how do we determine what to save and what to delete?"

"It's a quandary," he said, sipping his coffee. Lindsey gave him a side-eye. Was he making fun of her? He turned and met her gaze, and then batted his eyelashes, making her laugh. She had endured a three-day-long boat show for him last summer, which had left her mind-numbingly bored. She couldn't fault him if he felt the same about this.

"Off topic, and maybe I misheard, but did Derek say something about murder?"

"He did. I heard him, too," Sully said. "I get the feeling he's seen a thing or two."

"You don't think he actually meant someone would murder a person over that first edition Highsmith, do you?"

Sully thought about it for a second. "Nah. I mean it's cool and all, but it's not like it's an illuminated manuscript from the late-fifteenth century. Comparatively, who would murder someone over a mystery from the nineteen fifties?"

"Oh, you just referenced the program we attended on the train ride here," Lindsey said. She clasped her hands over her chest. "So you really don't mind when I drag you to these things and then go on and on about the history of books?"

"Of course not," Sully said. "You light up when you talk about your musty old books. How could I not listen?"

Lindsey sighed. And that right there was why she'd married him.

Sully put his arm around her shoulders as they made their way through the crowd to the next talk. "Don't worry about the book. I'm sure the director will find its rightful owner."

"You're right," she said. "The librarian in me just has to let it go."

As they made their way down the hallway to the next discussion, she noticed that everyone they passed was carrying a conference tote bag. The book she'd found could belong to anyone. How would Penny ever find them? And how could a person just lose a book like that? It boggled.

CHAPTER

2

BRIAR CREEK
PUBLIC LIBRARY

"A re all of your things stowed?" Sully asked.

They were settling into their roomette on the train back to New Haven, and Lindsey checked that she had put her carry-on, tote bag and shoulder bag securely in the storage space on the upper bunk so they didn't get knocked around.

"All put away," she said. "And you?"

"Same," he said. He patted his bag on the shelf beside his seat.

The roomette they were booked into consisted of two seats that faced each other and could be broken down into a bed, which was where Sully was sleeping, since he was the larger of the two of them, while Lindsey slept in the bunk above, which lowered from the ceiling and could be accessed by a couple of steps built into the side of her seat.

It was cozy, and she had loved sitting in her chair on the journey to Chicago from Briar Creek, reading while the snowy landscape passed by. When the conference had been announced with this year's location being Chicago, the planners had taken a quick survey of attendees and discovered that many were planning to arrive by train, and a discount was offered as well as some onboard conference programming, including the opening night lecture on illuminated manuscripts.

Lindsey didn't think Sully would be interested in taking the train, but with his love of all things with engines, he'd admitted that he'd always wanted to travel by rail. His enthusiasm had won her over, and she'd agreed. The trip had been a very pleasant surprise, plus it was so convenient, as they could board the train right in Briar Creek.

When she added turndown service from their car attendant Patrick and complimentary coffee, the train won the travel battle hands down.

"Ready to go grab dinner?"

"Yes!" Lindsey cried. Realizing she sounded very enthusiastic, she added, "I think the lake effect cold has fueled my appetite. I mean, I love to eat and all, but I'm abnormally starving tonight."

"Me, too," Sully said. "Let's get to the dining car before it fills up."

He led the way out of their snug little room. The train rocked slightly beneath their feet, and Lindsey held on to his arm as they made their way through the passageways of several more cars until they reached the dining car.

Until they had taken the train from New Haven to Chicago for the conference, Lindsey had never traveled by rail for anything longer than day trips to New York or Boston. There was a train station in their small village, but the train did not stop there as regularly as it did New Haven's Union Station, which was the closest large station.

The dining car was surprisingly only half full. They found a table for two by a window. Their server, dressed in a suit jacket and tie with a name tag that read *Sam*, handed them menus and then poured them each a glass of water from a pitcher. Lindsey was impressed that he was able to do this so smoothly.

"Wine?" Sully asked her.

"Yes, please," she said.

He ordered her favorite, a chardonnay, and a beer for himself. Night had fallen, and there was no scenery other than the lights of the towns and cities they passed through, each growing dimmer as they entered a more rural stretch. The rumble of the train engine became a background noise that Lindsey filtered out as she studied their fellow passengers.

She saw several people from the conference, including Penny Minton, Henry's harried assistant, who was sitting at a table for two on the opposite side of the car. She was seated with a man who was leaning over the table and talking animatedly. Judging by the flush in her cheeks and the sparkle in her eyes, she was having a lovely time.

The man appeared to be around the same age as Penny, whom Lindsey guessed to be about thirty. He was wearing a gray-and-black-plaid sports coat over a white dress shirt, his dark hair looked in need of a trim as it curled at his collar, and his beard was equally unkempt.

Still, he was smiling at Penny as if he enjoyed her company, and Lindsey hoped that was the case because, judging by what she'd observed at the conference, working for Henry did not seem like a great deal of fun. The man said something in a low tone, and Penny burst out laughing. Her lips parted in a wide, warm smile and she lowered her head and put her hand over her mouth as if to stifle the sound of her laughter. The man's smile was appreciative, as if he enjoyed being the cause of Penny's amusement.

"Husband? Boyfriend?" Sully asked. Lindsey glanced at him and noted he was studying Penny and her companion as well.

"I'm not sure he's a boyfriend yet," Lindsey said. "There is a freshness about them, a getting-to-know-you vibe, as if they haven't been acquainted that long. Also, there's no ring on her finger, so that rules out a fiancé or husband."

"Assuming she's the sort to wear a ring," Sully agreed. "But you're right, they do seem to be in the early stages. She certainly looks happier now than she did while on the receiving end of that dressing-down from Standish."

"Henry has a reputation for being difficult," Lindsey said. "Which might have contributed to the abrupt shift in careers for him."

Sam, their waiter, who appeared to be in his early twenties with a ready smile and a bounce in his step, arrived with their beverages, and they placed their dinner orders. Having never eaten in the dining car on a train before this trip, Lindsey was looking forward to it, as the food had been excellent on their way to Chicago. They decided to share an appetizer, a Mexican street corn soufflé, before their soup and salad course. Lindsey had chosen the rigatoni Bolognese for dinner, while Sully went with the flat iron steak, cooked medium rare.

"When you said Henry had a career shift, it sounded as if it wasn't by choice."

"It wasn't," Lindsey said. "He was working as the curator of Holden Barclay's private library on the Upper East Side of Manhattan. Barclay's an eccentric billionaire whose collection is his obsession. When Barclay asked for an outside appraisal to be done for insurance purposes, the appraiser discovered some of the original works that Henry had acquired for the collection were forgeries."

Sully let out a low whistle. "You said Standish was difficult. Was he about that?"

"Yes." Lindsey lowered her voice in case someone could hear them over the steady hum of the train. "He accused the appraiser of trying to steal his job and besmirch his reputation. He threatened to sue her for slander and vowed to ruin her career."

"And did he?" Sully asked.

Lindsey shrugged. "If he did, nothing came of it. Lydia Armand was the appraiser in question and, interestingly enough, she did take Henry's position as curator after he was fired."

Sully's eyebrows drew together and his brow furrowed. "That seems suspicious from an outsider's perspective."

"Oh, it was suspicious from all of the insiders' perspectives, too," Lindsey said. "Like Henry, Lydia had an impeccable reputation in archivists' circles but not after she replaced him."

"Why? Wouldn't she have been heralded as the good guy in this scenario, given that she outed someone who either knowingly committed fraud or was fooled, proving his abilities to be less than stellar?" Sully asked.

"You would think so," Lindsey said. "But there were a lot of hard feelings that the position was never opened to other professionals, and that it was just given to Lydia."

"Ah," Sully said. "I can see where that would irritate."

Lindsey sipped her wine and nodded. "A few of my colleagues at the time were very upset."

"Did the furor die down afterward?"

"It might have, but the forged items in question disappeared shortly after the hullaballoo. I think that's how Henry managed to get the directorship for the conference. He said that the fact that the items were stolen was very convenient for Lydia and that her entire appraisal was suspect and that he believed that she did it specifically to get rid of him. The archivist world at large felt badly for Henry, and they collectively turned on Lydia."

"What happened to her?" Sully asked.

"As far as I know, she still works for Barclay in his private library," Lindsey said. "There was some very malicious gossip about her having an affair with Barclay, but I find that hard to believe."

"Why?" Sully asked.

"Because he's much older than her," Lindsey said. She leaned across the table and lowered her voice. "And Lydia is a very attractive woman."

They paused while Sam delivered their appetizer. They each picked up their fork to tuck into it.

"Do you think that's why Barclay hired her? Is he a womanizing sort of older man?" Sully said. He took a bite of the soufflé and nodded. "Really good."

Lindsey dug her fork in and lifted a bite out. She watched the steam rise and said, "I don't know if Barclay is a womanizer. I've never seen him. He's very reclusive and seldom leaves his penthouse. I only know what I heard about him when I was working at the university. He drove a lot of the archivists crazy because he'd scribble his initials, H.B., in pencil on the endpapers of all his books. They were certain it would decrease the value, but they also speculated that he simply didn't care. He has a compulsion to mark things as his, and he is ruthless about getting what he wants."

"In what way?"

"He's known for being unscrupulous when it comes to acquisitions. He outbids universities, museums and other affluent bidders, and then he takes the materials into his private vault, never to be seen again." She tasted the soufflé and said, "That's delicious."

"What sort of materials does Barclay collect?"

"Shakespeare folios, Egyptian papyri, Mesopotamian tablets," Lindsey said. "You name it, he's snatched it. Ruffled some feathers of foreign governments while he was at it, too."

"Why would Standish or Armand work for him?" Sully asked. "I mean, doesn't it go against their academic standards to assist someone who keeps materials in a private collection away from scholars?"

"I can't say for certain as I don't know either of them very well, but I think they had to believe that by working for Barclay, they might have an opportunity to make him reconsider his hoarding tendencies," Lindsey speculated.

"And how has that worked out?"

"Judging by that fact that no one has ever seen his collection other than the lone archivists who work for him, I'd say not well," Lindsey said.

"Would you ever take a job like that?" Sully asked. He was studying her as if he'd discovered a new layer to her of which he'd been unaware and was charmed. Lindsey felt herself get a bit flustered under his bright blue gaze. Married over a year and he could still make her feel special. She hoped they always felt this way about each other.

"Back when I was studying to be a preservationist, I'd have jumped at the chance for a job like that," she said. "But I like to think that once I realized what a hoarder Barclay was, I'd try to gain access to his collection in order to convince him to lend it out. Sort of like a spy for the resistance, if that makes sense."

"It does, and I can absolutely picture you doing just that." Sully lifted his glass and clinked it against hers. "Too bad Standish and Armand didn't handle the job that way."

"Maybe they tried and failed," Lindsey said. "I don't imagine it would be an easy task to talk a billionaire hoarder into sharing their treasures." She sipped her wine as she studied her fellow passengers. Her gaze strayed back to Penny. "I wonder if she found the owner of the Highsmith book. I suppose it would be bad form to interrupt her date and ask."

Sully's knowing gaze met hers. His look was affectionate and he asked, "Do you really think you'll be able to sit here through an entire meal and not ask her?"

Lindsey sighed. "I'm not sure whether I'm flattered that you know me so well or embarrassed."

"No need to be embarrassed," he said. "Of course you want to know if she found the owner. The librarian in you has to be concerned."

"Thank you for not calling me nosy," Lindsey said.

"Never that," Sully said. A smile tipped the corner of his lips, and she knew he was teasing her.

She would have called him on it, but the sliding steel door at the end of the car whooshed open, letting in a blast of cool air. The woman who entered walked with the confidence of someone who knew that everyone in the room, or in this case the train car, was looking at her. With her burgundy coat with the faux leopard collar and a matching hat with the same fur trim, Lydia Armand strode down the aisle as if she owned the entire train.

"Well, I'll be," Lindsey muttered.

"Be what?" Sully asked. He turned to see whom she was looking at.

"Damned," Lindsey said. She leaned across the table and whispered, "That's her. That's Lydia Armand."

A low murmur rippled through the car as heads swiveled to watch her. Lydia seemed oblivious as she chose an empty table and slid into a seat with all the grace of a runway model. Lindsey half expected her to pull a cigarette case out of her handbag and wait for all of the men in the dining car to rush forward with a light. Yes, she was just that glamorous.

Lindsey glanced across the aisle at Penny Minton. Her eyes were wide behind her thick-framed glasses, and her mouth formed a small O. Her fork was raised halfway to her mouth as she'd clearly forgotten what she was doing with the arrival of Lydia.

"This might be an understatement of epic proportions," Lindsey whispered to Sully. "But I think things are about to get very interesting."

CHAPTER

3

BRIAR CREEK
PUBLIC LIBRARY

Lydia shed her coat, crossed her legs and picked up her menu. She settled comfortably into her seat as if completely unaware of the hissing whispers that had erupted at her arrival. Lydia was older than Lindsey had thought. Fine lines creased the corners of her eyes and her jawline sagged a bit, and yet she was still a stunning woman to behold. Lindsey thought it was the air of confidence she exuded. A person could live their whole life and never have that much presence.

The car door farthest from Lindsey and Sully opened, and Henry Standish strode into the dining car. He didn't look anywhere but at Lydia, as if he already knew she was here, and was coming fully prepared for a showdown.

Lindsey glanced at Penny to see if she was surprised by

her boss's appearance. She wasn't, and she had her phone in her hand, so it was clear she'd given him a heads-up.

"You!" Henry yelled at Lydia with all the contempt and disdain he could pour into the pronoun. "What are you doing here?"

Lydia didn't acknowledge him in any way. She merely continued to peruse the menu. Sam waited patiently by her table as she questioned him about whether the Bolognese was plant based. Sam said it could be, and he carried on, refilling waters and chatting with the other diners seemingly oblivious to the tension in the car. Lydia continued to ignore Henry. Lindsey suspected it was a power play to try to aggravate Henry. From the look of the throbbing veins in his neck, it was working.

Henry stomped down the aisle between the tables. His face was mottled, his hair looked as if it had lost a battle with the wind, and the blue scarf around his neck was dragging longer on one side than the other as if it was barely hanging on to his person.

"I know you can hear me, Lydia. What are you doing here?" he demanded.

Lydia didn't glance up from the menu when she said, "Yes, I can hear you. I imagine the entire dining car can. Don't be a bore, Henry. There's no need for a scene."

"No need?" he cried. He blinked at her. "You ruined my reputation. You stole my job. I'd say there's every reason for a scene."

"I'll have the baked salmon, but be sure my salad arrives

first with the dressing on the side," Lydia said to Sam. "And a glass of pinot noir, please."

"Yes, ma'am." He collected her menu and turned to Henry. "Will you be joining the lady?"

Henry made a choking sound as if he'd just swallowed a bug. "I wouldn't sit with that two-faced snake in the grass if it was the only seat available on the entire train!"

Sam glanced between them with wide eyes. "Okay, then." He turned and headed for the exit as if relieved to put some distance between himself and whatever was about to happen.

"Do sit down, Henry," Lydia said. She waved at the empty seat across from her. "You're being tedious."

Henry didn't sit. Instead, he stood bristling like a dog who'd been left out in the rain. "I will not. Tell me why you're here."

"I'm going home," Lydia said. "Much like everyone else, I expect."

Henry's eyes narrowed. His voice when he spoke sounded outraged. "Were you at the conference?"

"Of course," she said. She glanced up at him with a close-lipped smile. "It's the annual conference. I wouldn't miss it. You outdid yourself this year."

"This year?" Henry looked like he was on the brink of apoplexy. "You've come before?"

Sam appeared with Lydia's wine. She took the glass off the tray and toasted Henry. "Of course. I never miss it."

"But how?" Henry asked. "I would have known. I would

have seen your name. I would have seen you." He waved his hand at her as if she was something to be avoided at all costs.

"And canceled my registration no doubt," Lydia said. "That's why I don't use my real name."

Henry gaped at her. Lydia, unperturbed, sipped her wine.

"Penny!" Henry cried.

Lindsey saw Penny jump in her seat. Her companion frowned, clearly not happy that her boss was calling for her in such a strident tone.

"Yes, sir?" Penny rose and hurried forward. Her flushed happiness from moments before disappeared, leaving her looking pale and anxious.

Lindsey felt the same flash of concern for her as Penny's companion. She didn't want to see Henry take his displeasure at Lydia's appearance out on his assistant.

"Did you know that she was registered for the conference?"

"No." Penny shook her head. "I would have told you."

Henry planted his hands on his hips and glowered at Penny. "Would you? Would you really?"

"Yes, of course," Penny insisted.

"Maybe you were bribed to look the other way?" Henry asked. He narrowed his gaze as if reconsidering everything he'd ever known about his assistant.

"Henry, you're making a spectacle of yourself," Lydia said. "Again."

"No one is talking to you," Henry snapped. He turned back to Penny. "Tell me the truth."

"I am," Penny insisted. "I would have told you if I saw Ms. Armand's name on the list of attendees, I swear."

"Really? Then how is she here?" Henry asked.

"I don't know," Penny said.

She sounded utterly bewildered, and Lindsey felt her own protective instincts rise up. She glanced across the table and noticed that Sully had turned in his seat. He was ready to wade into the fray if need be. Penny's companion beat him to it. He rose from his seat and stood behind her.

"I think you're being horribly unfair, Mr. Standish," the man said.

"He's right," Lydia agreed. This only provoked Henry into a bigger fit.

"So that's how it is," Henry snapped. He stepped forward, glaring at the man standing behind Penny. "You think I don't know who you are? Kirk Duncan, collector of mid-century first edition noir."

"You're a collector?" Penny asked her companion. "Why didn't you tell me?"

"It hadn't come up yet," Kirk said. "I wasn't trying to hide anything."

Penny bit her lip, looking conflicted.

"That's right," Henry railed. "He's trying to romance that book we found right out from under you."

"What?" Kirk cried. "I was not. I am genuinely interested in Penny as a person."

"Sure you are," Henry scoffed. "Did you tell him about the rare first edition, Penny?"

"I—um," Penny stammered.

"Of course you did." Henry waved a dismissive hand. "And he was suddenly interested in you afterward, wasn't he?"

Penny hung her head, her face red with embarrassment. She took a small side step away from Kirk, and Lindsey felt her heart pinch. It was all just so cruel.

"You obnoxious little toad." Kirk stepped forward and stared Henry down. "Just because you don't see the value in a woman as smart and interesting as Penny doesn't mean the rest of us are so oblivious."

"You tell him," Lydia cheered Kirk on. She raised her glass in a toast and took a long sip.

Henry let out a guttural growl and balled his hands into fists.

Lindsey turned to Sully. "Do you think Lydia and Henry are going to get violent?"

"Eh, could go either way," he said. He reached across the table and squeezed her hand. "Don't worry. We won't let it get to that."

Lindsey knew that by *we* he meant him, since he was the one with military training, but she appreciated being counted all the same.

"Value?" Henry cried. "She's only interesting to anyone because she's my assistant."

Penny flinched as if he'd slapped her. She backed away until she'd reached her table and grabbed her handbag from her seat. "Excuse me," she whispered as she fled from the car.

"Penny!" Kirk called after her. He looked genuinely distraught. He turned back to Henry. "You are a revolting human being, and I am going to do everything in my power to see that you are removed as the conference director."

Henry laughed. "And how do you think you're going to make that happen?"

Kirk stepped forward until he loomed over Henry. "You got two things right. I am Kirk Duncan and I do collect midcentury first edition noir. But you missed one little detail."

Henry tipped his chin up. "What? That you have a soft spot for spinster secretaries?"

"No." Kirk smiled at him, but it was without humor or warmth. "My grandmother happens to be Jasmine Bellamy."

Henry's defiant stance deflated as swiftly as a balloon pricked by a pin. He licked his lips, and his gaze shifted from side to side as if he expected this Jasmine Bellamy to leap out at him from somewhere.

"Oh, Henry, you arrogant ass." Lydia laughed. "Now you've done it. Jazz is the acting president of the Archivist Society. She can have you removed from your position like that." Lydia snapped her fingers to emphasize her point.

"She won't," Henry said. His voice was uncertain, wobbling a bit in the middle, making it clear he was nervous.

"Won't she?" Kirk asked. He looked Henry over. "I'm going after Penny, and you'd better hope she's more forgiving of you than I am."

Henry looked as if he'd argue but then thought better of it. Kirk stormed out of the car in the same direction Penny had taken. The other diners turned back to their meals, but

Lindsey kept her gaze fixed on Henry and Lydia. She suspected they weren't done.

"If you didn't bribe my assistant, then how did you attend the conference without anyone recognizing you?"

"You didn't really think you could blackball me, Henry, did you?" Lydia asked.

He lifted one eyebrow in response, indicating that, yes, he'd actually thought that.

"I'm aware that you've made me persona non grata, but you can't shut me out of our profession completely. As for your conference, I simply attended under a fake name and wore the very unassuming attire of the average middle-aged woman, you know, the ones who at the age of fifty become invisible to the world at large for some inexplicable reason," she said.

"Why?" he asked. "Why would you do that when you know you're not welcome?"

"Perhaps I'm not, but there were people I needed to see and things I needed to . . . acquire," she said.

Sully turned back around to face Lindsey. He gestured that he was still listening, and she nodded, indicating she was, too. She supposed it was rude to eavesdrop, but it wasn't as if the two of them were making it that difficult with their raised voices. Besides, she wanted to hear if they mentioned the book she'd found.

There was something suspicious about how it had been left under her seat. She wondered if someone had stolen it from another conference goer but then panicked, fearing they were about to be caught, so they stuffed it in the nearest place they could find and hoped to get it back again later.

"Acquire? Such as what?" Henry asked. His voice dropped and his hostility ebbed. It was clear he was intrigued as to what Lydia was buying for his former boss.

"You know," Lydia said.

"I'm afraid I don't," he argued. "There were some very valuable pieces for sale at the conference."

"Pfft." Lydia made a dismissive noise. "I'm not talking about the vendors. I'm talking about a midcentury novel, inscribed by the author to the famous movie director who made a film out of her book. It was supposed to be in the silent auction."

Lindsey's eyes went wide. That was the book she found! It had to be. Sully's eyebrows shot up as he reached the same conclusion. For a beat they sat there staring at each other, waiting to hear what Henry said.

"I have no idea what you're talking about," Henry said.

"You're a terrible liar," Lydia said. "You turned a one-of-a-kind item, which was removed from the auction at the last minute, over to your assistant as if it was nothing. You screwed up, Henry. Again."

"The item to which you're referring was removed from the auction by the donor, which was why it was left off the final auction roster," Henry said. He gave her a condescending glance. "Did you not keep up with the auction updates? It wasn't the only item removed, and we had several new ones added. It happens every year."

"You returned the book to the donor, then?" Lydia asked.

Lindsey held her breath, waiting for his response. She'd only seen the final roster for the auction, which was why she hadn't known it was originally an auction item. That would have been useful information to have. There was a pause, as if Henry was trying to decide what to say. Lindsey wanted to jump in and demand answers. Instead, she fiddled with her utensils.

"Do you really think I'm going to share any information with you?" Henry asked. He stiffened his spine. "You forget I have no interest in you or what you think, and you have no business questioning me about how I manage the business of the director of the conference."

A slow smile spread across Lydia's very red lips. She glanced at Henry from beneath her eyelashes and said, "Unless I decide to take that job away from you, too."

Henry gasped as if she'd threatened to steal his firstborn. "You wouldn't dare!"

"Wouldn't I?" she asked. She put down her glass and rose to her feet. She had a good two inches on Henry, and she used them to look down her nose at him. "The truth is you're in over your head. You can't manage the conference any better than you curated Mr. Barclay's collection. You need to be put out to pasture, Henry."

"Are you comparing me to an old racehorse?" he snapped.

"You're right," she said. "That's unfair . . . to the horse."

"That tears it!" Henry cried. "I will see your membership in every professional archivist society is rejected."

Lydia feigned a yawn.

Henry bristled. She was clearly getting to him. "You think you're so special. Just because you stole my position—"

Lydia crossed her arms over her chest and glared. "I didn't steal anything. You were incompetent, spending a small fortune on fraudulent items because you were too lazy to verify their provenance."

"I had proof!" Henry yelled. His face was red and his breathing sounded as if he'd just run a mile uphill.

"And yet when the moment came to provide certificates of authenticity, you couldn't find them or the items to which they belonged," Lydia said. One jet-black brow rose up on her forehead. "How very convenient."

"For you, you mean," Henry hissed. "I could have proven their worth, but suddenly they were no longer in the vault." He paused and took a deep breath as if considering what he was about to say, and then a calm came over him, the sort of calm a high diver exhibits right before jumping off the platform. "Wouldn't it be extraordinary if one of the items that went missing just happened to land in my possession again?"

Lydia stared at him for a beat and then said, "It would certainly make it easier to have you arrested for fraud."

Henry glowered. "I've listened to enough." He stepped back and looked her over as if assessing her worth and finding her lacking. "We're done here. Do not ever cross my path again."

"Are you threatening me?" Lydia asked. She put a hand on her chest and blinked at him as if shocked by his malevolence.

Henry stepped forward and lowered his voice. "I'd say it's more of a promise. I know you and I know what you're capable of. Watch your back, Lydia."

"I don't think I'm the one who needs to," she said. "I'm coming for you, Henry."

A flash of fear crossed Henry's face. He took two steps back and then turned and fled the car in the same direction Penny and Kirk had taken. Lydia watched him go and then sat down at her table. She sipped her wine and then took out her phone. She began scrolling through it as if the uncomfortable altercation hadn't just happened.

Slowly the conversational buzz in the dining car resumed. Sam delivered their meals to Lindsey and Sully, and they thanked him. Lindsey stabbed the rigatoni with her fork. Her appetite was no longer her main concern.

"Well," she said. She didn't know what else to add. Lydia was sitting nearby, and Lindsey didn't want to be a gossip, but still.

"Agreed," Sully said. "I don't even know what to make of all that. There's clearly still a lot of bad blood there."

"I had thought it might have faded over the years," Lindsey said. "But now that I've seen the hostility between them up close, I have to say wow. That was tense."

She took a bite of her pasta. It wasn't Monteverde, but it was still very tasty. The sauce was flavorful and the noodles weren't overcooked. Sully cut into his steak, looking satisfied as well.

"What were the fraudulent books that went missing while Henry was curator?" Sully asked.

Lindsey shrugged. "No idea. They were never mentioned by title, just that they were suspected to be replicas, and then they went missing, putting Henry in the weird position of not being able to prove their worth and vindicate himself or have them be evaluated as frauds and be exposed as incompetent."

"Which is why he was allowed to be the director?" Sully asked. "Because there was no proof?"

"Essentially," Lindsey said. "I remember my boss at the university was against his appointment as conference director. She felt that the missing items were suspicious."

"Sounds like his successor feels the same," Sully said. "How well do you know Henry Standish? Do you think he could have been duped by fraudulent materials?"

Lindsey shook her head. "I don't know him well at all, only in passing, as we belong to the same archivist societies and such. I think what always bothered me about the situation was that Henry couldn't track down the source for the materials he'd purchased. That would have been a simple way to clear his name, but he said he couldn't remember who the book dealer was. That never sat right with me."

"How much money did he pay this book dealer whose name he can't recall?" Sully asked.

"Exactly!" Lindsey cried. "We're talking thousands of dollars of materials. If I wrote a check with someone else's money for that sort of investment, you'd better believe I'd remember their name, where they lived, the name of their first-grade teacher and what their first pet was. I'd be worse than the three security questions you have to answer online, you know, the ones you can never remember the answers to."

Sully laughed. "Oh, yeah, whenever I get asked for my favorite sports team, I panic. I mean, it depends upon what season it was—baseball, hockey or football—when I answered the question originally."

Lindsey nodded. "Just like you wouldn't think a person would have more than one favorite color, but some of us do."

"Again, it depends upon the season," he said. His eyes glinted with humor when his gaze met hers, and Lindsey knew that her husband understood her completely. It was an incredibly comforting feeling.

"Excuse me." Sam appeared at their table. He looked nervous, and Lindsey smiled, trying to put him at ease. "Is everything satisfactory?"

"Yes," Sully and Lindsey answered together.

"Good, um, the thing is, Ms. Armand would like a word with you," he said. He gestured with his hand in the direction where Lydia sat, and Lindsey wondered if he was afraid to look at her. Interesting.

She glanced past Sully and saw Lydia staring at her. Lindsey had to resist the urge to look around as if there had to be someone else whom Lydia Armand wanted to speak with, as it couldn't possibly be her.

"Of course," Lindsey said. She reached for the napkin in her lap and dabbed at her lips. She glanced at her husband and said, "I'll be right back."

Before she could slide out of her seat, Lydia appeared at

their table. Sam glanced at her and then Lindsey before he cautiously backed away.

"Oh, don't get up." Lydia waved her hand. "I just have a few questions for you. You're Lindsey Norris, yes?"

"Yes," Lindsey said. "This is my husband, Mike Sullivan."

"Charmed," Lydia said without taking her gaze off Lindsey. Her stare was intense as if she was trying to assess Lindsey.

"How can I help you?" Lindsey asked.

"It's nothing to worry about. I'm just gathering some facts." Lydia's lips curved up in a smile that didn't light her eyes. "You're the woman who found the first edition of *Strangers on a Train*—how appropriate given where we are—aren't you?"

CHAPTER

4

BRIAR CREEK
PUBLIC LIBRARY

Lindsey glanced at Sully. How much should she share with this strange woman? He glanced from Lydia to Lindsey and then nodded. It was the same thing her instincts had told her. She wanted to know what Lydia knew, and the only way to discover that was to admit that she was the one who'd found the book.

"Yes," Lindsey said. "It was in a bag under my seat at Brooklyn Wainwright's lecture on book restoration. It was a fascinating talk—"

"I know. I was there," Lydia interrupted.

"Oh," Lindsey said. She wasn't sure what else to say under Lydia's hard, assessing stare. "I had Brooklyn take a look at it, and she gave it a cursory assessment of great value, given its condition and being signed by the author to one of the most famous filmmakers of all time."

"Hmm." Lydia tapped her chin with her index finger. "And then you gave it to Standish?"

"Yes," Lindsey confirmed.

"And he gave it to his assistant, Penny Minton."

"That's right." Lindsey nodded. Despite Lydia's intimidating presence, Lindsey reminded herself that she was only attending the conference to brush up on her skills, since the library had recently acquired a rare collection of first editions. She no longer worked as an archivist, so whatever Lydia thought of her was irrelevant. "May I ask why you care?"

"My employer Holden Barclay is interested in the book," she said. "If it's authentic and the condition is as described, it will only increase in value. It would be a wonderful addition to his already exemplary collection."

"Did you come to the conference for that book specifically?" Sully asked.

Lydia glanced at him. "Among others. That particular volume was to be sold in the silent auction held on the opening night of the conference, but when the auction began, the book wasn't included. Henry insists the anonymous donor pulled the item at the last minute, which happens sometimes, but then it appeared under your chair."

She tipped her head to the side, and Lindsey got the feeling she was debating whether or not Lindsey had something to do with the item's sudden appearance. She tried not to squirm.

"It seems strange that Standish didn't seem overly alarmed that a missing auction item was found when Lindsey turned it over to him," Sully said.

"He did say it was of particular interest." Lindsey frowned. She remembered feeling as if there'd been a subtext to the conversation between Henry and Penny.

"Not that Henry cares. He is only interested in regaining his standing in the community," Lydia said. "I doubt he realized that the book you found was the one that was supposed to be auctioned. That's why he was a terrible curator. The devil is in the details, and he wanted none of that."

"I noticed he didn't answer you when you asked him if the book had been returned to the donor," Lindsey said. "Do you think he's hiding something?"

"Other than his own incompetence?" Lydia asked. She turned and stared at the door through which Henry had departed, before turning back to Lindsey. "I don't know, but I will find out. Enjoy your dinner."

With that she returned to her seat, moving with all the intention of a runway model on the catwalk.

Lindsey reached for her wine. She leaned toward Sully and spoke in a low voice so that only he could hear. "That was exhausting. Just me?"

"No," Sully said. He lifted his beer and tapped her glass. "Let's just be glad that it has nothing to do with us. I don't think it'd be comfortable to be in the crosshairs of that woman."

"Agreed," Lindsey said. She took a bite of her dinner, which thankfully was still hot. "Do you think Henry returned the book to the donor?"

"My gut tells me no," he said.

"Mine, too," she agreed. "I wish I'd never found it. I

mean, I know it's a classic and the book itself, signed by the author for the filmmaker, is incredible, but the whole situation is stressing me out. Very Hitchcockian, actually."

They ate silently for a few minutes, and then Sully put down his knife and fork and leaned his elbows on the table. Lindsey recognized this as the stance he took when he had something important to say. She put down her fork and dabbed her mouth with her napkin.

"What is it?" she asked, leaning in.

"True confession time," he said.

Lindsey went very still. What could her husband possibly have to confess? She met his earnest gaze and felt a very small flicker of panic flutter in her belly. Was this deal breaker stuff? Was their marriage in trouble? No, that couldn't be it. Could it?

"I've never read *Strangers on a Train* or seen the movie," he said.

It took a moment for his words to sink in past her alarm. It was then that she noticed the twinkle in his eyes. She laughed and shook her head.

"Really, Sully?" she asked. Relieved and amused, she picked up her fork.

"I know. It's clearly an oversight on my part," he said. "Can you give me the short version of the story?"

"Absolutely," she said. "It's really ingenious. Although, the book and the movie are different. Highsmith's characters and plot are a bit darker."

"Than Hitchcock's?" Sully asked. His eyebrows lifted in surprise.

"Yes," Lindsey said. "The short version is two strangers meet on a train and one suggests that they each murder the other's nemesis, reasoning that neither of them would be a suspect because they are strangers. It was Highsmith's first novel."

"Impressive," Sully said.

"I won't tell you how it unfolds because you might want to read the book or watch the movie, and I don't want to spoil it for you," she said.

"We could watch the movie back in our roomette on your laptop," he said.

"Oh, that's perfect since we're on a train and all." Lindsey took a deep breath and felt her shoulders droop. She wondered if the missing book was on the train.

"You're thinking about the book again, aren't you?" he asked.

"The librarian in me is a little obsessed about what happened to it."

"Understandable," he said. "But maybe Penny found the original owner. We'll likely see her again, probably at breakfast, and we can ask when emotions aren't running so high."

"I'm not so sure. Coordinating a conference that big was a huge amount of work. I imagine the end of it requires them to decompress for a bit. If I were Penny, I'd never leave my compartment."

"I wouldn't blame her. Maybe she's in her sleeper car watching *Strangers on a Train* right now," Sully said.

"Maybe," Lindsey said. "If I don't see her, I can always reach out to her at the conference headquarters and ask."

"After the exchange she had with Standish, you might want to do it sooner rather than later," Sully said. He took another bite of steak, chewed and swallowed before he added, "I can't imagine she'd willingly keep working for a man who called her out like that in front of everyone."

"Definitely, as soon as we get back," Lindsey said. "Their offices are in New York, so they're only a few train stops beyond ours. She should be home no more than two hours after us, which would be midday tomorrow, meaning I could reach out to her the next day."

"Bright and early Monday morning," Sully said. "I'm sure she'll be happy to hear from you."

Lindsey forked up the last of her pasta and glanced at him. "Are you making fun of me?"

"No, never that," he said. Then he winked.

Lindsey smiled. She was very grateful Sully was here, otherwise she might get more obsessed than she already was, and the next thing she knew, she'd be badgering their car attendant Patrick to tell her which roomette Penny was in and then knocking on Penny's door, demanding to know if she had found the owner of the book. Yes, it was good that Sully was here to rein in her inquisitive impulses. The book had likely been returned to its original owner and Penny would confirm that when Lindsey spoke to her again.

Lindsey believed this was the likeliest outcome, and yet, as she glanced at the other diners, all of whom had resumed their meals, including Lydia Armand, she couldn't shake the feeling that something bad was going to happen. She tried to brush it off, but her gaze was caught by Lydia's piercing stare, and Lindsey felt the icy fingers of dread walk up her spine. It took everything she had not to shiver.

Instead, she reached for her wine, tossed her long curly blond hair over her shoulder and returned her attention to her husband. She could feel Lydia's gaze upon her as she sipped her wine, but she refused to react. She was not going to let Lydia Armand intimidate her. Whatever issues Lydia had with Henry were not Lindsey's concern, and she was going to keep it that way.

On their overnight to Chicago, Lindsey had been certain she wouldn't sleep. She'd been wrong. The rocking motion of the train and the sound of the engine had knocked her out, so she expected to be lulled the same way on their journey back to Connecticut. No such luck.

Sully, on the other hand, had no problem falling asleep even after they'd watched *Strangers on a Train*, which in hindsight wasn't the most restful choice they could have made.

Not wanting to disturb him, Lindsey read the latest Alaska Wild mystery by Paige Shelton and tried not to think about the missing Highsmith book, Penny Minton, Henry Standish, Lydia Armand or Holden Barclay. Halfway through a chapter, before the author could leave her on a cliff-hanger, Lindsey closed the book and switched out the light. She was just fading into sleep when she heard a thumping noise coming from the compartment next to theirs. She tried to ignore it but then heard the noise again.

She opened her eyes and stared into the darkness, wondering what was happening next door. Had the passenger fallen out of their bed? She glanced at the safety net on her bunk provided to prevent such accidents. What if that person hadn't adjusted theirs properly? Were they injured? Should she call the car attendant? She didn't want to disturb him if it was nothing. Maybe she should go knock on her neighbor's door and see if they were in trouble.

She slid out of her loft bed and down the narrow carpeted steps to the floor. Sully didn't stir, so she left him to his sleep. She was wearing flannel pajama bottoms and a thermal top, which were not exactly revealing. She grabbed Sully's hooded coat, knowing it was likely to be chillier out in the passageway, and she bent over to slip on her shoes. When the jacket's hood slid onto her head, she left it there, liking the anonymity of covering her hair and face given that she was a woman and it was the middle of the night. She crept to the door and pulled the heavy curtain aside. She couldn't see anyone in the passageway. She waited a beat to see if she heard the noise again.

There was another ominous thump and the sound of a door slamming shut. That decided it. She unlocked the door and slid it open. Standing at the end of the passageway was a figure in a long black coat. They wore a black hat over their hair, and a scarf covered the lower half of their face. Their eyes were the only thing visible, but they were so far away she could barely see them. The person stood sideways as if they'd been in motion but Lindsey's appearance had interrupted them.

"Everything all right?" she asked.

The person nodded once but they didn't move, as if they were waiting for her to go back into her compartment. Lindsey stepped back. She wasn't getting a threatening feeling from the person exactly, it was more like an unsettling one, and she didn't want to be out in the hallway alone with them.

"Good night," she said. She opened the door to her roomette and stepped back inside, closing it behind her.

"Are you okay, darling?" Sully, groggy with sleep, lifted his head from his pillow.

"I'm not sure. There's a person out there."

Sully, to his credit, didn't point out that they were on a train full of people so finding a person in the hallway wasn't unexpected. He knew her well enough to know if she mentioned the person it was because something felt wrong.

"I'll check it out," he said. He rolled up from his bunk, wearing the same flannel pajama bottoms and thermal top as Lindsey. His sister, Mary, had gotten everyone in the Sullivan family a matching set for Christmas, and they had the holiday jammies photo to prove it.

Sully stepped into his shoes and moved beside her. Lindsey shrugged out of his coat and handed it to him. "It's chilly in the passageway."

He slipped it on and opened the door. Lindsey grabbed her coat and pulled it on, and they both leaned forward and peered out. Lindsey glanced up and down the narrow hallway. The person in black was gone. Sully stepped into the passageway, and she followed.

Lindsey studied the sleeper compartment doors. All of the roomette doors had windows with navy blue curtains on the inside. Every single curtain was drawn, even the ones in the room next to hers and Sully's.

There was no noise coming from that sleeper, and she debated knocking just to make certain the occupant was okay. It was after midnight, however, and she hated to disturb them if they were sleeping. She stood, staring at the door trying to decide what to do.

"I also heard some strange noises coming from next door," she said. She pointed at the closed door with the curtain drawn. "It's all quiet now, so I'm not sure if I should knock or not."

"Did you hear a cry for help?" Sully asked.

"No, just some thumping," she said. "I thought maybe they fell out of their upper bunk."

"Do you want me to knock?" he asked. "It could be that they just dropped something."

A door opened down the passageway and a head poked out. "What's going on out here?"

It was Lydia Armand. She had her black hair pulled back with a wide headband, and a bunch of gold cosmetic patches covered her face, one under each eye and one between her eyebrows.

Startled, Lindsey wasn't sure what to say. "Nothing."

Another door opened, and Penny Minton squinted at them. She fussed with the pocket of her robe, pulling out her glasses and slipping them onto her nose. "Is everything all right?"

Lindsey felt her face get warm. Now they were in the middle of a scene. "No, no, sorry if we woke you."

A compartment at the end of the car opened, and Kirk Duncan appeared. He was wearing a bathrobe over his pajamas and carrying a toothbrush. "What's going on? Penny, are you okay?"

She ignored him.

Another man stepped out of the shower room at the end of the car. Like Kirk, he was wearing a bathrobe and carrying a shaving kit. Lindsey recognized him from the conference. He'd been at Brooklyn's talk and had asked some very insightful questions.

"Are we having a late-night party?" the man asked. "Should we take it to the bar car?" He was tall and broad, good-looking with a neatly trimmed beard and matching head of dark hair cut in a very precise high-and-tight style.

"It's after midnight," Lydia snapped. She glared at Lindsey and Sully. One of her skin patches drooped. "Or don't you care that the rest of us are trying to sleep?"

"I—" Lindsey began but Sully interrupted.

"Sorry, it's my fault," he said. He sent Lydia his most disarming smile. "I thought I heard some worrisome noises coming from our neighboring compartment and came out to check. Didn't mean to alarm anyone."

"Apology accepted. Now keep it down out here." With that Lydia disappeared back into her room, slamming the door behind her.

Lindsey watched as she yanked her curtains over the

window with a bit more force than seemed necessary. She glanced at the others and shrugged.

"Good night," Penny said on a yawn and disappeared.

"Good night," the man at the end said. "Call me if you change your minds. I'm always up for a drink."

"Penny, wait," Kirk said. She didn't wait but closed her door right in his face.

Despondent, Kirk walked to his own compartment and closed the door.

Lindsey turned and faced Sully. "So, that was embarrassing. Thanks for taking the heat from Lydia for me. It was unnecessary but appreciated."

"No problem." He yawned and then pointed to the neighbor's door. "Want me to knock just in case?"

"No, I think I've caused enough of a ruckus," she said. "The banging noises were probably the person I saw in the passageway when I stepped outside. They appeared to be in a hurry, so maybe they tripped and fell or something."

"These cars do all look the same," Sully said. "Maybe they were just lost."

"Also, I think maybe the movie got into my head," she said.

Sully opened the door to their compartment, and she stepped inside. He adjusted the curtain and locked the door.

"It's been a very dramatic day," he said. "I'm sure when you get some sleep, you'll feel better."

Lindsey nodded. She kissed him and gave him a quick hug before she climbed back into her loft bed. Sully shut the lights out and within moments, she heard his deep, even breathing. She willed herself to relax and sleep, but it was impossible. She found her thoughts straying to the person standing in the passageway.

She couldn't decide if the passenger had appeared more ominous or frightened. Perhaps they'd just had too much to drink in the bar car and were having a hard time making it back to their compartment. The way they had stood in the passageway, staring at her from behind the black scarf. She couldn't help thinking that they were up to no good.

"Ugh," she mumbled. "No more Hitchcock movies before bed."

"Very wise," Sully said from below, making her start with a yelp.

Lindsey took an extra pillow from her bed and threw it onto her husband. He laughed and then said, "Good night, darling."

"Good night."

There was a pause and he added, "And stop thinking."

If only she could.

CHAPTER

5

BRIAR CREEK
PUBLIC LIBRARY

Their car attendant arrived with their morning coffee, and having not slept very well, Lindsey was extremely grateful.

"Hi, Patrick," she said. She slid the door to the roomette open.

"Good morning," he greeted her. On the other side of middle age, with no more than a few random tufts of hair left on his head, Patrick spoke with a faint Irish lilt and had a ready smile that he shared freely. He held a small tray with a silver carafe and two thick ceramic mugs accompanied by a small pitcher of milk and a bowl with all the packets of sugar Lindsey could want.

She stepped aside so he could place the tray on the small table that folded down between their two seats and she said, "You're a god among men, Patrick."

He laughed. "I'll take that. Is there anything else I can get you?"

"Not for me," she said. "Sully's stepped out but I'm sure he's fine, too."

"All right, then, just hit your call button if you need me," he said.

Lindsey blinked. That's right. They had a call button that went right to Patrick at all hours, day or night. She wondered if their neighbor making the thumping noise last night had used theirs.

"Patrick, did anyone use their call button last night, say, shortly after midnight?" she asked.

Patrick's eyebrows rose as if he wasn't sure how to answer that.

"I don't want to invade anyone's privacy, and you certainly don't have to tell me who, but I heard some noise last night from the roomette next door and I thought maybe they were in distress," she said.

Patrick frowned. "I can tell you this, if they had called me, I wouldn't mention it out of respect for their privacy, but since no one called me, I feel it's okay to tell you that. It was quiet as could be last night. Not one call."

"Huh." Lindsey nodded. "I suppose that makes sense. When I stepped into the passageway to check on them, the noise stopped and I didn't hear another sound all night."

"Hello, Patrick." Sully appeared in the open door to their compartment.

"Good morning, sir," Patrick said. "Your wife was just telling me that she heard some noise last night."

"She did," Sully said. "Unfortunately, I slept through it."

"Do either of you think there's cause for concern?" Patrick asked.

Sully glanced at Lindsey. She hadn't heard a cry for help last night, just someone thumping around, and they'd stopped, so she couldn't complain that they'd kept her awake. If she thought about it, they really had no reason to invade that person's privacy. She shook her head.

"All right, then." Patrick nodded. "If there's anything you need, don't hesitate to call me."

With a cheerful wave, he left them to carry on with his duties. Lindsey glanced at Sully. He was freshly shaved and smelled like he always did, of the sea and sun. She had no idea how he managed that when they'd been cooped up in a train for almost twenty-four hours, but he smelled like home, and she gave him a quick hug.

"Do you think Patrick thinks I'm a busybody?" she asked. She poured them each a cup of coffee and they took their seats, facing each other beside the window.

Sully drank his coffee black, and he blew across the surface of the mug, sending the steam from the hot coffee into the air. Lindsey added milk and sugar to hers and took a bracing sip.

"No, he doesn't, because you're not," he said. "You heard some disturbing noises, it's only natural that you'd be concerned."

"I still say I got *Strangers on a Train* in my head, and it made me paranoid," she said.

"It was a pretty great movie," he agreed. "Which would you say is better, the movie or the book?"

"I'm a librarian," she answered.

"And?"

"I think it's part of the official code of conduct for librarians that we have to say the book is always better than the movie. Always."

Sully laughed. "I can see the dilemma, but there has to be a movie out there that's better than the book."

"*Die Hard*," she said.

"That was based on a book?"

"See?"

"Point taken."

Lindsey continued, "The movie was based on a book by Roderick Thorp called *Nothing Lasts Forever*, but I think Alan Rickman and Bruce Willis made the movie version incomparable, but if you tell any librarians I said that, I will deny it."

"I would never." He toasted her with his coffee cup, and they enjoyed their hot beverages while watching the winter scenery pass.

"Any idea where we are?" she asked.

"According to the app on my phone, we're approaching Boston, where we'll stop at South Station, and then it's a little less than two hours to home."

"So we have time for breakfast?"

Sully nodded. "Apparently, the waffles are amazing."

"Waffles?" Lindsey rose to her feet. She picked up her laptop bag, planning to do a little work during breakfast. "Let's go."

She was only joking, mostly, but they still hurriedly finished their coffee and made their way to the dining car.

When the door slid open, Lindsey noted that it was full to bursting. So much for working while she ate breakfast. There wasn't enough room available to sit with her laptop open.

The smell of coffee and bacon perfumed the air, and she felt her stomach growl. She scanned the room, looking for people she knew that they could join. Unfortunately, she'd left behind the archivist world a few years ago and wasn't as well connected as she used to be. There was no one from her old job in the dining car, nor was there anyone she knew from her days at library school.

"Are you looking for seats?" a voice asked.

Lindsey turned to see the man who'd come out of his roomette and asked if they were having a party last night just before Lydia yelled at them. He was seated at a table for four all by himself. He had papers spread all around him, which he began to gather.

"We don't want to disturb you," Lindsey said.

"You're not," he replied. "If you sit with me, I'll be required to make polite conversation instead of working, so believe me, you're doing me a favor if you join me."

Lindsey smiled and noted that Sully did, too. "In that case, thank you."

"Very generous of you," Sully said.

They took the two seats opposite their dining companion. He was dressed casually this morning in jeans and a
gray T-shirt with a thick hooded navy blue sweatshirt over
it. He glanced out the window as they got settled, and said,
"I hear there's snow in the forecast."

"That won't impact the train, I hope," Lindsey said.

"No, it's supposedly a light snow, and even if it wasn't,
most train systems put severe weather plans in place months
in advance," the man said. "I'm Andrew Shields, by the
way."

"Nice to meet you," Lindsey said. She reached across
the table and shook his hand. "I'm Lindsey Norris and this
is my husband, Mike Sullivan."

"But everyone calls me Sully." The men shook hands.

Sam appeared beside their table. He handed Sully and
Lindsey menus and said, "Your breakfast will be right out,
Mr. Shields. Can I get you all coffee or juice?"

"Coffee, please," Lindsey said. Sully ordered the same,
and Andrew asked for a refill of the empty cup in front
of him.

"I'm glad I ran into you two," Andrew said. "What happened last night that had everyone out in the passageway in
the middle of the night?"

Lindsey glanced at Sully. She had no idea how much she
wanted to share about hearing noises and then getting
Lydia all riled.

"I mean I know I came out because that dark-haired
woman was yelling," Andrew said. "Otherwise, I don't think
I would have heard a thing."

"She was yelling because of me," Lindsey said. "I heard some noises and went out into the passageway to check it out, but they stopped."

"What sort of noises?"

"Loud thumping sounds, coming from the compartment next to ours."

"Thumping noises?" Andrew asked. "Like someone falling out of their bed?"

"Exactly!" she cried.

"Which was why we were having a debate in the passage about what to do," Sully said. "I mean, everyone has a right to privacy, but if they'd gotten hurt, then we felt we should check on them."

"But as Patrick reminded me, there are call buttons in each compartment," Lindsey said. "If someone was in trouble, wouldn't they just call the car attendant for help? Unless, of course, they couldn't."

"I can see why you were debating," Andrew said. "People can be awfully prickly about their privacy, especially these days with social media and cameras recording everyone and everything all the time."

Sam stopped by their table with their coffee and a pot to refill Andrew's. The conversation lagged while he took their orders, but once he'd left, Sully turned to Andrew.

"You look familiar to me. Were you at the archivist conference?" he asked.

"I was," Andrew said. "I was about to say that you two look familiar to me, too."

Lindsey nodded. "That's because we were all at the

book restoration panel. I remember you asked some very insightful questions."

"Thank you," he answered. "I'm new to the field, but I like to think I'm a quick study. I've found that you can learn a lot just by being observant."

"Agreed," Sully said. "Not paying attention to your surroundings can get you killed."

"I imagine you do a lot of weather watching, working outside all day like you do," Andrew said. He sipped his coffee while Sully sat up straighter, a frown marring his forehead.

"What makes you think I work outside?" Sully asked. Lindsey was glad he did, because she was curious, too.

"You have the look of a man who spends his life outdoors," Andrew said. "You're fit, your hair is lighter on the ends, probably from the sun, and I can see where your tan, which appears to have faded a bit with winter, ends at your shirt collar. You're either a professional golfer or a man who works outdoors."

"I'm a boat captain, actually," Sully said.

"Well, that actually does sound exciting." Andrew grinned. He glanced at Lindsey and said, "And you're clearly a librarian."

"How did you know?" she cried. "Do I look like a librarian? Not that there's anything wrong with that."

"It was actually just a guess because of the conference," Andrew said. "It's a noble profession, being the keepers of knowledge. Did you know that one of the occupations most common to *Jeopardy!* contestants is librarian?"

"We do consider that bragging rights," she said. "There has to be some reward for keeping all of this random knowledge lodged in our heads. Still, that was a very good guess."

"Full disclosure," Andrew said. "It wasn't a guess so much as deductive reasoning, since I saw you talking to Brooklyn Wainwright after the panel on book restoration, and most of the people in her audience were librarians, so that clinched it."

"Well, that disappoints," Lindsey teased.

Andrew grinned again.

"Were you at the conference on behalf of work or for yourself?" Sully asked.

"A little bit of—" Andrew broke off with a glance behind them. "Hang on to your seats. Here comes the angry woman from last night."

"Is anyone sitting there?" Lydia stopped by their table. She dropped her conference tote on the ground and took the seat beside Andrew.

He scooted to the side, affording her more room. Lydia said nothing but stared at Lindsey. "Have you seen Henry this morning?"

"No," Lindsey said. "Should we have?"

"No, I mean I suppose he's sleeping in after what I'm sure he thinks was a tremendously successful conference," Lydia said.

Sam appeared beside their table and delivered Andrew's heaping plate of eggs and breakfast meat.

"Coffee," Lydia barked at Sam. After a beat, she added, "Please."

"Of course, Ms. Armand," Sam said. He looked as if he was afraid of her, which Lindsey completely understood. She was a bit afraid of Lydia, too.

Sam handed Lydia a menu and departed. She stared at it with a small frown between her brows. Lindsey got the feeling that Lydia was studying the menu but not really seeing it. As if to verify this, Lydia slapped the laminated sheet down and stared around the dining car.

She turned and studied Andrew. "And who are you?"

Andrew turned from his plate with his fork halfway to his mouth. "Oh, we're going to observe the social niceties now?"

Lydia waved a dismissive hand at him. "I'm Lydia Armand, curator of the Holden Barclay collection."

"I know," Andrew said. "You made quite an entrance in the dining car last night."

She narrowed her eyes at him, clearly waiting for him to introduce himself.

Lindsey felt her anxiety spike. An introvert by nature, she had never found social gatherings to be enjoyable, and when there was tension, she wanted to flee. She thought longingly of her roomette with the view of the New England shoreline. She glanced out the window and saw snatches of the water through the trees. It settled her.

Andrew took the bite off his fork that had been suspended, and thoughtfully chewed and swallowed, chasing it down with a sip of coffee. Finally, he glanced at Lydia and said, "I'm Andrew Shields."

"And?" she asked.

"And what?" he asked.

"Were you at the conference? Are you a collector? A librarian? What?" She fired the questions like a drill sergeant.

"Why do you want to know?" he asked.

"Because most of the train is made up of people who attended the conference, many of whom want Henry's position as director of the conference," she said.

"Including you?" Lindsey asked.

Lydia turned her fierce gaze on Lindsey, and she felt her core muscles clench as if anticipating a blow. To her surprise, Lydia laughed.

"I have less than zero interest in Henry's job, but I like to make him think I want it just to torture him," she said. "No, there are plenty of others who are gunning for that thankless job."

She jutted her chin in the direction of their fellow diners. She pointed an impressively long and lethal-looking red fingernail at the passengers. "Scott Westinghouse, director of the rare book and manuscript library at the Cross Foundation, known mostly for being a womanizer and a raging alcoholic. He and Henry loathe each other, as he competed for Henry's position as conference director and lost."

Lindsey glanced at the man across the aisle. Westinghouse was middle-aged, with a solid paunch, receding hairline and small rectangular glasses. He looked like a generic corporate white dude. He also had his mouthful of scrambled eggs, which everyone could see as he laughed at something his companion, a woman young enough to be his daughter, said.

"And that's Sally Kilpatrick." Lydia gestured to a woman seated farther down the car. She was also middle-aged, with gray corkscrew curls that reached her shoulders, a deep brown complexion, and lively dark eyes that lifted and met Lydia's gaze directly. After a moment, Sally raised her cup of coffee in Lydia's direction in acknowledgment.

"Truthfully, Sally would be an amazing conference director," Lydia said. "She's very good at grassroots fundraising, is an excellent public speaker, and could shift the conference to focus more on the profession than herself, unlike Henry."

"Where does Sally work now?" Lindsey asked.

"A private women's college in North Carolina," Lydia said.

Sam arrived with her coffee and Lindsey's and Sully's breakfasts. Lydia ordered dry toast and a plain yogurt, and Sam darted away.

Lindsey looked at the waffles on her plate heaped with fresh fruit and whipped cream. She refused to feel guilty that she was eating a calorie-loaded plate of yummy goodness while Lydia had ordered a breakfast that made Lindsey suspect that Lydia hated herself on some innermost level.

"My point," Lydia continued, "is that I know just about everyone who is on this train who attended the conference, but I don't know you, Mr. Shields. So who are you?"

Andrew picked up a crisp brown slice of bacon and bit

into it. He chewed contemplatively, and Lindsey suspected he was enjoying making Lydia wait for his response. She tapped her long nail on the table impatiently. Lindsey didn't think she imagined that Andrew chewed even slower. She glanced at Sully, and he sent her a quick wink, letting her know he was watching their companions, too.

"I'm new to the book profession," Andrew said. "Although, I have worked with rare materials before. I attended the conference mostly on behalf of my employer."

"A private buyer?" Lydia's thinly shaped eyebrows rose.

"Something like that," he said.

"Who?"

"I'm not at liberty to divulge that information," Andrew said. He sounded regretful, but Lindsey doubted that he actually was.

"What was this collector interested in?" Lydia asked. When Andrew started to shake his head, she spoke quickly. "I might be able to help you. I am the curator of the greatest private collection in the Northeast, after all."

Andrew picked up his fork and speared a sausage. "I doubt it," he said. "Since the item I was sent to acquire was withdrawn from the silent auction and later found shoved under a seat at a panel."

Lindsey gasped. "The Highsmith book."

"Correct," Andrew said. "My employer will not be pleased that its current whereabouts are unknown."

Lydia stared at Andrew with a narrowed gaze. "I would assume that Henry and his assistant managed to return the item to the original owner."

"You know what they say about assuming, it makes an ass—" he said.

"Yes, yes, I'm familiar." Lydia held up her hand to stop him.

"Does anyone know who the owner is?" Sully asked.

Both Lydia and Andrew shook their heads, and Andrew said, "Anonymous was the only information I could get."

"There's a person who might know." Lydia pointed at the end of the train car.

They all turned to look. Penny Minton entered through the sliding door with Kirk Duncan right behind her.

"Just leave me alone," Penny hissed as she made her way down the aisle. She was scanning the tables, looking for a seat.

"Not until you hear me out," Kirk protested. "Penny, you haven't spoken to me since Henry accused me of only being interested in that stupid book."

She stopped trying to leave him behind and whirled around. "Aren't you though? Isn't that why you approached me initially?"

Kirk opened his mouth and then closed it. Lindsey's heart pinched for Penny.

"That's what I thought," she said. She turned and slid into the seat beside Sally Kilpatrick, who reached over and patted her shoulder in a comforting way.

Kirk skulked to the last remaining vacant seat at the end of the car.

"You know, it is surprising that Standish isn't here," Andrew said. "This is the perfect place for him to do his victory lap at the end of a conference, and I'm surprised he'd miss that."

"I'm sure he's exhausted," Lydia said. "His moment in the sun is over until next year."

Lindsey frowned. While she didn't know Henry personally, she knew him professionally, and she thought Andrew was right. Being out and about and soaking up all the praise and adulation seemed more his speed.

"I think Andrew's right," Lindsey said. "I wonder where Henry is."

"He was staying in the compartment next to yours," Andrew said.

"I'm sorry, what did you say?" Lindsey asked. She felt her heart thump hard in her chest.

"Henry was staying in the compartment next to yours," he repeated. "I saw him go there after dinner last night. Did you not know?"

"No, we didn't," Lindsey said. She turned to Sully with wide eyes. Suddenly, she had a very bad feeling about the noises she had heard last night. "We should check on him after breakfast, don't you think?"

"Can't hurt," Sully agreed.

Sam arrived with Lydia's breakfast.

"Ouch!" she cried. "You stepped on my foot."

"I'm so sorry, Ms. Armand," Sam said. He looked like he was about to drop the coffee carafe, but Lindsey grabbed it from him while Sully took the plate of plain toast. Sam was left holding the bowl of yogurt.

"You could have broken my toe." Lydia bent over to

examine her foot. She fussed for a moment and then popped back up. "My shoe, my very expensive Jimmy Choo, is scuffed but otherwise it's fine."

"Are you sure there's nothing I can do for you?" Sam asked. He swallowed visibly as if he expected her to ask for his head on a platter. She didn't. Instead, she took up her coffee cup, dismissing him as if he were a pesky housefly.

"No, I'm fine, but you need to be more careful," Lydia snapped.

"I will be, I promise." Sam put down her yogurt and practically ran from their table. Lindsey didn't blame him a bit.

CHAPTER

6

BRIAR CREEK
PUBLIC LIBRARY

I t had to be Henry I heard last night," Lindsey said as they made their way back to their compartment.

"Assuming Andrew is correct about where he was staying," Sully said. His voice was the calm balm to the panicked note in Lindsey's. "I mean, he could be wrong and it could be someone else's compartment."

"Maybe, but it is very out of character that Henry wasn't in the dining car for breakfast," Lindsey said.

"Perhaps, or maybe Lydia is right and he was just exhausted from planning a conference for a year and now that it's over, he's sleeping in," Sully said. His tone was reasonable, but Lindsey's gut wasn't having it.

"We have to check," she said.

"Of course," Sully agreed. "But let's not panic—yet."

After hastily finishing their breakfast, Lindsey and Sully

had left their companions in the dining car and hurried back to their roomette. Lindsey kept replaying in her head the thumping noises she'd heard last night, wondering if Henry had fallen or hurt himself and hadn't been able to call for help. She'd never forgive herself if she could have helped him but didn't.

"No matter what we discover, you can't blame yourself," Sully said. Her husband knew her so well. "There was no way to know what happened in the compartment next to ours."

"Hmm," Lindsey hummed noncommittally. Sully reached for her hand and gave it a reassuring squeeze.

They stored Lindsey's bag in their compartment and then stepped back into the passageway. They paused in front of the compartment assumed to be Henry's and exchanged a look. With a nod, Lindsey raised her fist and knocked on the glass. It was a gentle knock. There was a part of her that was still nervous about disturbing whoever might be inside. They waited a beat. There was no response.

Sully lifted his eyebrows, and then he raised his fist and rapped on the door. It was much more forceful than Lindsey's had been, and she was certain that if it was Henry inside he must have to have heard him. Still, there was no answer.

"What should we do?" she asked. "We can't break the door down."

"I'll use our call button to summon Patrick," Sully said. "Wait here and keep an eye on the door in case Henry answers. I'll be right back."

Lindsey nodded, and Sully slipped into their compartment. She pressed her face against the window of the door, trying to peer inside. The curtain was drawn, however, and she couldn't see a thing. She hoped Andrew was wrong and the car was actually vacant. Maybe the person she'd seen in the hallway last night was someone leaving this compartment to get off at their stop. The train had stopped frequently on their journey, and the thumping noise she'd heard could have been someone's bags.

She frowned. Except the person she'd seen in the passageway last night hadn't had any bags. She glanced at the door to her compartment, wondering if Sully was able to reach Patrick.

The door whooshed open at the end of the car, and Penny entered the aisle. She had her hands in her pockets, and her shoulders were hunched. Kirk was right behind her, still pleading his case.

"Penny, I'm telling you the truth," he said. "Just give me a chance."

"Even if I wanted to, which I don't," she said. "The whole thing is pointless. I'm getting off the train in New York, and you're going on to DC. We live in two different worlds, and I think it's just better that way." She paused in front of her compartment. "Have a nice life."

She was about to enter her roomette, when Sully popped out of theirs and said, "Patrick is on his way, and he said given the situation, he'd be all right with opening the door to the compartment."

His voice brought Penny's attention to them. "Are you having someone open Mr. Standish's compartment?"

Lindsey pointed to the door in front of her. She'd been hoping Andrew was wrong. "This is Henry's roomette? Are you sure?"

"Given that I booked the tickets, I am," Penny said. She stepped around Kirk and approached them. "Why? Is something the matter?"

"Our breakfast companion pointed out that Henry wasn't in attendance, but it seemed like the sort of event Henry wouldn't miss after closing such a successful conference," Lindsey said.

Penny worried her lower lip between her teeth. "That's accurate." She glanced at Sully. "Is that why you were out in the hallway last night? The noises you heard came from Mr. Standish's room?"

"Yes, we believed so, but we didn't know it was his room at the time," Sully said.

"I should have realized last night that you were talking about his compartment, but I was preoccupied," Penny said, shooting an annoyed glance at Kirk as if this was somehow his fault. "And Ms. Armand was so furious, I wasn't processing things very well."

"None of us were," Lindsey said. "Otherwise I would have called for Patrick last night and had him check."

"Could Standish have already left the train?" Kirk asked.

"But why would he? He lives in New York, and we're not there yet," Penny said. "And you're right, Mr. Standish is the sort who loves the afterglow of an event. It was one of the reasons that the train travel option held so much appeal for him. He planned to visit with everyone who attended the conference and soak up all of the positive feedback."

There was a noise at the end of the car, and Patrick came out of the compartment on the end. He was in his usual vest and tie over a white shirt. He approached with a purposeful stride. At the same time the door on the opposite end opened and Lydia arrived with their breakfast companion Andrew right behind her.

"Oh, you're entering Henry's compartment?" Lydia asked. She walked faster. "Good. I have some questions for him."

Patrick glanced around at the faces of the gathering crowd. Lindsey met his gaze and said, "Sorry."

"No problem at all," Patrick assured her. He tried to open the door, but it wouldn't budge. "That's odd. It's not locked, but it won't open."

He turned to the compartment and knocked. Again, there was no answer. Patrick stepped back and glanced at the door. "Look at that. Someone put a shim between the door and the wall so it can't be opened." He wiggled it out, and the door slid open, and Lindsey glanced over his shoulder into the room. The compartment was in utter disarray, with clothes and papers strewn all over the small space.

"Mr. Standish," Patrick called his name.

"Henry, get out here," Lydia demanded in her usual no-nonsense voice.

There was no answer. Lindsey took in the mess that was his compartment and knew something was wrong. No one in their industry was this messy. There was a natural rage for order that consumed archivists and librarians, and while they might accumulate a lot of clutter, they weren't messy. Not like this. This was next level. It looked almost as if there'd been a fight.

Lindsey glanced at the floor. It was then that she saw the hand beneath the blanket that had been tossed onto the ground. She grabbed Sully's arm and squeezed, then pointed and said, "Look at the floor, I think . . ."

She didn't want to say it. She didn't want to say that she thought Henry might have fallen from his loft bed.

Patrick stepped forward and gently lifted the blanket off the person beneath it as if he were asleep and he didn't want to wake him. Lindsey supposed Henry could have gone on a drinking bender and be sleeping it off on the floor, but it seemed unlikely.

As Patrick removed the blanket, however, Henry was revealed. He was collapsed in a heap with his head bent at an odd angle. His skin was pasty pale, and his eyes were open and staring at them. A small trickle of dried blood ran from the corner of his mouth to the floor beneath him.

Lindsey gasped and clapped a hand over her mouth. Sully immediately put an arm around her and pulled her close.

"Mr. Standish!" Penny cried. She stumbled back, away from the open door, and Andrew stepped forward and caught her in his arms. She burrowed her face against his shoulder, and he led her away out of view of Henry.

Lindsey glanced at Lydia. Her dark eyes were flat, staring

at the scene in front of her as if she wasn't surprised but was also very unhappy. Kirk Duncan stood behind her, his mouth agape as he took in the scene. He paled and turned a sickly shade of green.

"Excuse me," Kirk said. "I think I'm going to be ill."

He charged down the passageway to the bathroom, where they heard him retch even after the door closed.

Lindsey glanced back into the compartment and noted that the upper bunk had been lowered and the netting that was provided to prevent a person from falling out of their bunk was in place on the outer side of the bed. How could Henry have fallen over it to the floor below? It was impossible.

Patrick had dropped to his knees beside Henry. "Mr. Standish?"

Henry didn't respond. Patrick felt for a pulse on the wrist of Henry's outstretched hand, then beneath his jaw. Unsatisfied, he put a hand on Henry's rib cage as if hoping to feel it rise and fall with breath. He leaned down and put his ear to Henry's chest.

After a few moments, which felt agonizingly long, Patrick turned a stricken face to the group and said, "I'm so sorry. It seems Mr. Standish has passed."

Penny let out an anguished sob and clung to Andrew, who patted her back while he stared over her head into the room, as if trying to determine what had happened to land Henry on the floor of his roomette. Lydia shifted her weight from foot to foot, and Duncan failed to reappear.

Even before Patrick declared him dead, Lindsey knew

that Henry had died from what was clearly a broken neck, but somehow hearing the words made her woozy. She felt her stomach roil and she turned to Sully.

"Now can we panic?" she asked as she leaned against him, seeking comfort.

"Yes," he said as he pulled her into a hug. He lowered his head so that only she could hear him. "Given the high possibility that there's a killer among us, now is a perfect time to panic."

CHAPTER

7

BRIAR CREEK
PUBLIC LIBRARY

Patrick sealed off the room with Sully's help. While Sully and Lindsey stood watch with Tom, the attendant from another car, Patrick went to speak to the engineer. They were halfway across Connecticut, and the train couldn't keep going. They were going to have to stop and deal with the body of Henry Standish and the very real probability that his death had not been an accident.

An announcement came over the intercom that all passengers were to report to their seats or their compartments. No explanation was given, but Lindsey suspected they'd be stopping soon. Since they were close to home, she decided to go pack.

She told Sully as much and squeezed his arm as she passed him to enter their roomette. He patted her hand but didn't follow her. Instead, he remained outside with the other attendant, who was young and looked nervous about his assigned task, while they awaited Patrick's return.

The door closed behind her, and Lindsey glanced out the window at the passing scenery. Winter in New England could be magical when fresh snow covered the ground and the trees, and everything was blanketed in a soft wintry hush, or it could be relentlessly gray, bone-chillingly cold and dreary. As she watched the barren landscape, leafless trees, yellow marshes and a steely gray sky fly by her window, she felt the oppressive scenery weigh her down. The snow that had been forecast wasn't arriving until later in the day, and at the moment things felt gloomy with a side of terrible.

She hadn't really known Henry, and what she'd seen of him over the past few days hadn't made him particularly likable. Still, he was dead. She had likely heard him die, and she'd done nothing. No, she didn't really think there was anything she could have done to stop it given that she didn't even know how it happened, but a relentless feeling of guilt assailed her anyway.

She thought about the way he'd been found, crumpled on the ground like a piece of refuse someone no longer needed. Had he fallen? Or had someone helped him to his end? There were clearly enough people on board the train who wished him ill, many of whom were very vocal about their dislike for him.

Then she remembered the person in the long black coat standing in the passageway shortly after she'd heard the thumping noises coming from Henry's compartment. Had they had something to do with Henry's death? Could they be his killer? Was that why they had disappeared the second she stepped back inside her own compartment last night? Were they worried that Lindsey might recognize them and turn them in? She felt her skin prickle. She did not want to get on the bad side of a murderer. She had been there before and it was not fun.

The door to the compartment opened, and she jumped. She whirled around to see Sully standing there.

He opened his arms and she stepped into them. "I'm sorry about Henry."

Lindsey nodded against his shoulder. "Me, too."

They were quiet for a minute and then Lindsey asked, "What happens next?"

"Believe it or not, we're stopping at the next town with a train station, which happens to be Briar Creek," he said. "They've already called ahead to inform the police, local and state."

"Are they going to investigate?" Lindsey asked.

"I imagine they need to determine whether he died of natural causes or not," Sully said. "And I'm sure they're going to question all of us. I suspect we're in for a very long day."

"I don't think he fell out of his bunk," Lindsey said.

"Because the netting was still in place?" Sully asked. "I thought the same thing."

"What about Patrick? What does he think?"

Sully shrugged. "Patrick didn't say anything. He's pretty shook up. He confessed he's never had a passenger die on him before, so he's feeling a bit out of his element. He and Tom are keeping watch over the compartment until we stop and the authorities arrive."

"Poor Patrick," Lindsey said. "The first dead body is the worst."

They moved to sit in their two seats opposite each other while the scenery rolled by. "I've been thinking about the noises I heard last night."

"And?"

"If I'm right and he didn't fall, then I believe he was attacked and I think he must have known the person who did it, otherwise why would he have let them in?"

Sully blew out a breath. "After listening to Lydia at breakfast, it sure seemed as if there were a lot of people who had a problem with Standish, and most of them are on this train. There's also the possibility that it's someone not on the train but with enough power to have put someone on the train to do their dirty work for them."

"Like a professional hit?" Lindsey asked. "Who would do that to an archivist in charge of an annual convention?"

Sully ran a hand over his face. "The former boss whose money he spent? Someone who wanted his job? Maybe someone he acquired materials from who felt they got cheated? Not to mention the fact that some of these books are insanely valuable. I imagine there are people who would kill to put them in their collections."

"And then there's the personal connections. Lydia certainly hates him, and his own assistant Penny must have some disgruntled feelings toward him. He might have pushed her right over the edge with his public cruelty yesterday."

"Or Kirk," Sully said. "He certainly defended Penny and threatened to have Standish fired by informing his grandmother of his displeasure with Henry."

"Not to forget the people Lydia pointed out at breakfast," Lindsey said. "Sally Kilpatrick and Scott Westinghouse both had issues with Henry, and those are just the people we know about. He clearly did not make a lot of friends in the industry."

Sully sighed and pressed his back into his seat. He tipped his head up, studying the underside of the bunk. "What is the most common motive for murder?"

"From what I've read about crime, particularly murder, the three most popular reasons to kill someone are greed, sex and power," Lindsey said. "How do we apply that to Henry?"

"Let's start with greed," Sully suggested. "Did Henry own anything of great value that someone would kill for?"

Lindsey shrugged. "I don't even know if he still had possession of the Highsmith book. We'd have to ask someone who knew him much better than I did."

"Sex, then," Sully offered. "Could Henry have had an affair gone wrong? Was he married and cheating? Maybe he was being stalked or stalking someone else?"

Lindsey pondered the possibility. "I don't know of any Mrs. Standish or Mr. Standish, so I don't think he was married. Penny referred to the compartment as being just his, so I assumed he was traveling alone, but it might be worth asking around to see if he had a companion on the trip. If so, where are they?"

Again, Lindsey thought of the person in the passageway. "Could the person I saw in the passageway last night have been involved with Henry? Maybe they had a fight and Henry falling was an accident?"

"Perhaps," Sully said. "But I think if Henry was involved with someone, other people would have known about it. Penny at the very least would know. She was his assistant, after all."

"I need to talk to her," Lindsey said.

"Are we getting involved in this, then?" Sully asked. To his credit, he kept his voice neutral, not giving Lindsey any indication of how he felt about it.

"Not involved, but there's no way I can avoid telling our chief of police and the state police or whoever is going to be investigating this murder about the noises coming from Henry's compartment on the night he died," she said. "And the person I saw in the passageway right after the noise stopped."

A shiver rippled down Lindsey's spine.

"That's true. You're involved to a certain extent whether you like it or not," he said. He looked grim but then reached forward and patted her knee. "It'll be all right. We'll handle it together."

"Thanks," Lindsey said. It was reassuring to have him in this situation with her. "Hopefully, they'll determine what happened sooner rather than later."

"Maybe it has to do with the last motive on your list," Sully said. "Power."

Lindsey tapped her chin with her forefinger. "That does seem probable. I mean, Henry had a significant amount of power as the director of the conference. He was the final say on who spoke, who attended, who was nominated for awards and so forth. And he certainly had no compunction about wielding his influence in favor of those he liked and against those he didn't."

"Like banning Lydia from attending?" Sully asked.

"Exactly," Lindsey said. "When a show of power is involved in a murder, it's usually the murderer exercising the ultimate power over their victim by taking their life."

"Which could come from a variety of scenarios," Sully said. "Like taking a job others wanted, bullying an assistant, exacting revenge on the person he thought wronged him. We . . . er . . . the police are going to have to find every person that Henry had a power play with and determine whether they were at the conference or on the train."

"When we had dinner with Emma and Robbie over the holidays, didn't Emma say that things had been quiet and she was bored?" Lindsey asked.

"I think she was hoping for a week in Hawaii with Robbie, not a murder on a train arriving in Briar Creek," Sully said.

"Perhaps she needs to be clearer about what she's manifesting when she says she's bored," Lindsey said.

Sully's lips twitched. "Please make sure I'm there when you tell her that. I want to see her reaction."

There was a knock on the door, and Sully rose and opened it. Patrick stood outside, looking edgy. "We're about to arrive at the Briar Creek station," he said. "I've been told that no passengers may disembark until the authorities have fully investigated the . . ." He waved his hand toward Henry's door. "Er . . . scene of the . . . er . . . incident."

Sully nodded. "That's as expected."

"The thing is, me and the police have a complicated relationship," Patrick said.

"Complicated?"

"I was a bit of a hooligan as a youth," Patrick said. "I've avoided any exchanges with them ever since."

"You've nothing to worry about," Sully said. "Chief Plewicki, Emma, is a friend of ours, and she's a straight shooter. She won't hold anything from your past against you."

Patrick visibly sagged with relief. "That's good to hear, but all the same, it'd be grand if you'd stay close."

"Absolutely," Sully said. He turned and glanced over his shoulder at Lindsey. She sent him a thumbs-up, letting him know that it was fine. She glanced out the window while Sully stood in the open door talking to Patrick. She could feel the train slowing and realized they had arrived in town.

The station for Briar Creek was not a frequent stop. The commuter train halted in the village only a couple of times in the morning and in the evening, and that was it. Any other time of the day and passengers had to go catch the train in New Haven.

The station was small, an old brick building that had once been a telegraph office on the edge of the village. Standing on the platform was Chief Plewicki with her second-in-command, Officer Kirkland, a big rawboned redhead who made for an intimidating presence on the police department staff, never mind that he was a genuinely nice person and would never harm a soul.

The train came to a complete stop and the doors opened. Emma stepped onto the train. She took one look at Sully and then behind him at Lindsey and sighed.

"Really, you two?" she asked. "You were gone four days and you come back with a body. You could have just brought me a T-shirt."

Lindsey smiled, relieved that Emma could make with the gallows humor. A man in a long black wool coat followed her onto the train while Kirkland stayed outside, presumably to keep anyone from entering or leaving the train.

Lindsey looked more closely at the man who followed Chief Plewicki. It was Detective Trimble, a detective with the state police whom Lindsey had worked with before when one of her staff members had been accused of murdering her boyfriend. His short-cropped black hair had acquired streaks of gray at his temples, but otherwise, he looked good.

"Lindsey Norris," Detective Trimble said. He adjusted his glasses on his nose. "This is unexpected."

"Hi, Detective," she said. "It's good to see you despite the circumstances."

"It would be nice to bump into each other at literally anything else," he agreed. Then he added, "Chief Plewicki said you've been an invaluable help to her over the past few years."

Lindsey looked at Emma in surprise.

"What? I can't give a compliment?" Emma asked as she pulled on a pair of blue latex gloves.

Detective Trimble did the same, and they turned toward Henry's compartment. Sully introduced them to Patrick, who looked calmer but still wary.

"Mr. Standish is in here," Patrick said. "We found him at nine fifteen this morning when Mr. Sullivan asked me to open his compartment because they were worried that he hadn't shown up for breakfast."

Emma nodded and gestured to the door. "All right, then."

Patrick unlocked the roomette and opened it. Lindsey watched Emma's face. Her lips tightened and her jaw clenched. Those were the only outward signs of her distress. Detective Trimble had the same shuttered expression on his face, and Lindsey supposed it went with the job.

Sully and Lindsey stepped aside, letting Patrick describe what happened when they'd opened the door. Both the chief and the detective examined Henry, and then they asked questions about the compartment. Who would have access to all of the compartments? Were there any security cameras? Had there been any disturbances in the night? That sort of thing.

Knowing it would be a while, Lindsey and Sully went back into their room, leaving the door open, and waited. Lindsey wondered what the other passengers were thinking. They had to be curious. As far as she knew, the only people who knew what had happened were those who were with them when they found Henry.

"Do you think they're going to keep the train here?" Lindsey asked. "I mean, they can't just carry on as if nothing has happened, right?"

"I imagine they'll have this car taken out of rotation while they investigate," Sully said. "The question is how are they going to question everyone on the train before they release them?"

Lindsey glanced out the window and noted that the snow had begun to fall and it was much thicker and fiercer than the light dusting that had been predicted. "Do you think the weather has turned? This seems like a much more powerful snowfall than expected."

Sully followed her gaze and his eyebrows lifted. "It does look like the beginnings of a blizzard. I suppose it'll depend upon how long it lasts."

"According to the latest weather reports, it's going to last all day and throughout the night," Emma said. She stepped into their car. "Which is why we're going to be inviting everyone on the train who was attending the conference and who lives out of state to bunk down in Briar Creek until the weather passes."

"By inviting, you mean . . . ?"

"It's an order," Emma said. "Both the state and the feds are involved in this investigation because we have no idea where the train was when our victim was murdered."

"It was definitely murder?" Lindsey asked. She was surprised to discover how much she'd been hoping it was an accident.

"Only the medical examiner can confirm for certain, and he's on his way, but judging by the defensive wounds on Mr. Standish's arms, my initial assessment is yes, he was murdered," Emma said.

Lindsey felt the air whoosh out of her lungs. She glanced at Sully and noted that he looked equally unsettled. She reached for his hand and squeezed it with hers.

Emma leaned against the doorframe. "What can you tell me about Henry Standish? Is there anyone who would have wanted him dead?"

"I can tell you who it wasn't." A voice spoke from behind Emma, and she whirled around.

Penny was standing in the passageway with her arms wrapped around her, her hair scraped back in a tight knot on the back of her head, her nose pink and her eyes red rimmed behind her glasses, indicating that she'd been crying.

"And you are?" Emma asked.

"I'm Mr. Standish's assistant," Penny said. "And I know everyone is going to think that I did it, but I'm telling you I didn't."

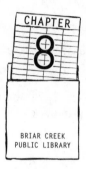

CHAPTER

8

BRIAR CREEK
PUBLIC LIBRARY

I f it wasn't you, then who do you think it was?" Emma asked. She turned her back to Lindsey and Sully and took a small recorder out of her pocket and pressed the record button. "Start by stating your name and how you know the deceased."

Penny took a deep breath, and with a voice that shook, she gave Emma the basics of her relationship to Henry. Then she recounted the career rivalry between Henry and Lydia, the hostility between Henry and Scott Westinghouse over the conference job, and Henry's absolute belief that his curatorial career had been ruined by his old boss Holden Barclay. Henry was obsessed with proving his innocence in the fraud scandal, and Penny believed that he was getting close and whoever wanted him to stay quiet had decided to make it permanent.

Emma listened intently. When Penny paused for breath, Emma asked, "And how was your relationship with Mr. Standish?"

There was a pregnant pause. Lindsey glanced at Sully to see if he was taking this in as well. He nodded his head ever so slightly.

"I don't know what you mean," Penny said.

"It's pretty basic," Emma said. "He was your boss. How did you get on?"

"Fine, completely fine," Penny said. She spoke quickly, defensively, and Lindsey knew that Emma noticed.

"Penny, what are you doing out here?" Kirk asked.

"I was telling the police about Henry," Penny said. "I was giving them a suspect list for his murder."

"I know you're upset, Pen," Kirk said. "But it was just an acc—"

"Exactly right," Lydia interrupted as she approached the group. "It was just a horrible, tragic accident."

Lindsey stood and glanced over Emma's head. Lydia was fully dressed in a long bright blue wool coat with a matching hat with black velvet trim. Her black low-heeled boots were perfect for this weather, and she towed a hard-shell carry-on bag behind her. She paused to pull on a pair of black gloves. With a tight smile, she made for the doors of the train car.

The doors slid open, and she prepared to step through only to find her way blocked by the very formidable form of Officer Kirkland, who stood in the center of the doors like a soccer goalie anticipating an incoming ball. No one was getting past him.

"Sorry, ma'am, but no one is leaving the train just yet," Emma said.

"Says who?" Lydia drew herself up and attempted to look down her nose at Emma.

"The Briar Creek chief of police," Emma answered as she stepped forward, standing right in front of Lydia while holding her gaze.

"Tell him some of us have work to get back to, and we don't have time for this," Lydia said.

"*She* doesn't care," Emma retorted. "Because she is me, and I don't care where it is you think you need to go. We have a blizzard knocking on our front door, a dead body in a train car, and no one is leaving town until I say so. Now you can either bunk up at a seaside inn or kick back in the town jail while awaiting questioning, which could take a very long time. These are your choices. Understood?"

Lydia took a moment to let her gaze run up and down Emma, from her wide-brimmed hat to her practical black boots. A flicker of respect lit her eyes, and she said, "You have one day."

Before Emma could respond, Lydia turned and towed her belongings back to her compartment. Penny glared after her, but Kirk looked thoughtful.

"If you would return to your compartments," Emma said to Penny and Kirk. "We'll be escorting you to an inn in town to stay overnight while we get things sorted. We'd like to get everyone settled before the weather gets worse."

"But I have to get home," Penny protested.

"No," Emma said. "This is a murder investigation. No one is leaving until Detective Trimble and I say so."

Penny stumbled back to her roomette, and Lindsey noted that Kirk went inside with her. She was relieved. Penny didn't look well and probably shouldn't be left alone at the moment.

"Just to clarify, we can go home, right?" Sully asked.

Emma turned back around and studied them. "Yes, but only because you live in town and the inn is going to be a tight squeeze as it is."

"And here I thought you were going to say it was because we couldn't possibly be suspects," Sully said.

"Everyone's a suspect." Emma turned and went to talk to Kirkland, who was waving at her.

Lindsey and Sully watched as the crime scene personnel arrived. They quickly donned their Tyvek coveralls and brought in their equipment. Lindsey recognized Dr. Rogers and Callie Bristow from a situation last autumn that involved the discovery of a body sealed in an airless room for over thirty years. She still had nightmares about the case, but the library had gained an amazing rare collection and Callie had become a regular library user; apparently she loved historical romance. Lindsey tried to focus on the positive.

"Hi, Lindsey," Callie said.

"Hi, Callie, it's good to see you," Lindsey answered. Then she cringed. Why did that feel like it had come out wrong?

Callie laughed. "Don't feel bad. We can compartmentalize our meeting from the unfortunate situation that brought us together, can't we?"

"Absolutely," Lindsey said. "Also, I just remembered that I have the new Loretta Chase novel in if you want me to put a copy aside for you."

"Yes!" Callie said. "This blizzard is made for fireside reading, and Chase always delivers."

Lindsey smiled.

"Bristow!" Dr. Rogers barked. "Were you planning on joining us in here?"

Callie grinned, clearly unrepentant. "Gotta go. I'll swing by the library in a few days."

"I'll be there," Lindsey said.

It took a while for the passengers who'd been at the conference to be separated from those who hadn't, and while one group was taken by bus to New Haven to catch the next train, the others were loaded into a school bus, provided by the town, to be taken to the Shores Inn.

"How did you manage to get the Shores Inn to house everyone?" Lindsey asked Emma as she and Sully stepped out of the train pulling their carry-ons behind them.

"I happen to know they had it booked out for a wedding today that got canceled at the last minute," Emma said. "Apparently, the bride walked in on the groom doing the deed with her maid of honor right after the rehearsal dinner last night."

"Oh, that's awful," Lindsey said.

"Yes, well, the bride managed to shellac the groom with a dropkick that was spectacular, and she was chasing down the half-naked maid of honor when we arrived. Not gonna lie, it felt wrong to take her in. Anyway, there's plenty of food, drink and vacancies at the inn, so that's where everyone is going."

"Waste not, want not," Sully said.

"Exactly," Emma agreed. "Besides, Michelle Brioni, you know, the woman who owns the inn, said she hated to send her staff home, as they were counting on the wedding to make some money. Now she can keep them on. Win-win."

"Since we're not staying at the inn, we need to call for a ride," Lindsey said.

"On it," Sully said, taking his phone out of his pocket.

"No need," Emma said. "I found one for you."

She gestured to the end of the platform where her boyfriend Robbie Vine stood with a flat cap on his head and a scarf about his neck. He waved, and Lindsey and Sully returned it.

"When he heard about the body on the train, there was no stopping him from coming to get you," Emma said.

"Of course," Lindsey said. "Robbie does love a good mystery."

"You are not to discuss the case with him," Emma said. Lindsey was about to protest, as she didn't see how it was possible to keep what had happened quiet in a village this small, but Emma raised her hand. "I know, but try. That man will get himself into the middle of things, you know he will."

"You're saying this to the woman who is known for getting herself into the middle of things," Sully said.

"I know," Emma said. "The irony is not lost on me."

"Robbie!" Lindsey called as they approached him.

"Greetings, weary travelers," Robbie said. He shook Sully's hand and gave Lindsey a quick hug. "Your conveyance awaits."

"How can he say the dorkiest things and still sound charming?" Sully asked Emma.

"It's the accent," Emma replied. "The man can get away with just about anything when he deploys that accent." Then she sighed.

"It's the number one weapon in my arsenal," Robbie agreed. "But I try to only use it for good."

Robbie was an actor who'd come to Briar Creek several years before, and after a near fatal run during the community theater production of *A Midsummer Night's Dream*, he had decided to stay. He'd become a close friend of Lindsey's, and after a time, he and Sully had put aside their differences, too. When he started dating Emma, the foursome had found they enjoyed one another's company and frequently got together for dinner or the occasional game night.

Sully and Lindsey put their bags in the back of Robbie's car. Sully opened the passenger door for Lindsey and then took a seat in the back. Robbie gave Emma a quick kiss and promised to be careful. The snow was getting thicker, and visibility was dimming.

"Looks like we arrived home just in time," Lindsey said. She squinted through the window at her neighborhood. The houses were small gray-shingled cottages built on quarter acres, leaving no room for the colossal homes that were being built on the larger lots in town. This suited Lindsey just fine.

She and Sully enjoyed working on their house together. He cooked, she cleaned, he did the laundry, she did the yard work. They shared the bigger remodeling jobs like staining the back deck to keep the salty sea air from rotting the wood. Their partnership was more than she'd ever expected out of life, and there wasn't a day that she wasn't grateful.

"How did the kids do while we were gone?" she asked.

"Well, I have ruined Miss Zelda," Robbie said. "She's mine now."

Lindsey laughed. "Can anyone ever really own a cat?"

"Heathcliff adores me, too," Robbie said. "But I think his heart will always belong to you."

"Thanks for watching them for us," Sully said. "Did it make you want a pet of your own?"

"I'd have a hundred pets in a heartbeat, but Emma won't let me." Robbie sighed. "She said until I retire and don't leave for work for weeks at a time, I can't have any pets because her schedule is too unpredictable and it wouldn't be fair to the animal."

"She's not wrong," Lindsey said. "I imagine she's going

to be logging a lot of hours at the inn during the next twenty-four hours."

"Speaking of the murder," Robbie began, but Sully interrupted.

"When did we mention murder?"

"It was in the subtext," Robbie said. He turned smoothly onto their street. "What exactly happened to the poor bloke on the train?"

"Do you have time for a cup of tea?" Lindsey asked.

"Always."

"Then come in and we'll tell you everything," Lindsey said.

Robbie turned in to their driveway and parked.

"Actually, I'm going to leave you to tell the tale, darling," Sully said. "I have a slew of texts from Ronnie at the office. The year-round islanders need some emergency supplies brought out, and if I want to get it done before the storm is worse, I'd better go now."

Lindsey glanced past their house out into the bay, where the archipelago known as the Thumb Islands dotted the horizon. Sully had grown up on one of those islands. He knew them as well as she knew the shelves in her library. But still she hated the idea of him out there during a blizzard.

"Be careful," she said. "And be quick."

"I have too much to live for not to be," Sully said. He kissed her and then climbed the three steps to the front door. "I just have to see the kids before I go. Brace yourselves."

Sully unlocked the front door and pulled it open. A ball

of fluffy black fur erupted out onto the portico. With a bark and a wag, Heathcliff stood on his hind legs and wrapped his front paws around Sully's knee in a Heathcliff version of a hug. Sully barely had time to scratch his ears before Heathcliff sensed Lindsey nearby. With a happy bark, he leapt off the front stoop, landing in an explosion of new-fallen snow, and bounded for Lindsey.

She had learned to brace herself for impact, but their days apart seemingly caused Heathcliff to be extra exuberant in his greeting, and despite her crouched stance, he took her down. The inches of snow that had already accumulated broke her fall, but the wind was still knocked out of her, and Lindsey lay there with Heathcliff standing on her chest, licking her face.

Sully and Robbie hurried forward. Their concern was tempered by their laughter. As Robbie hauled Heathcliff off her, Sully helped her to her feet.

"All right, darling?" he asked. He brushed the snow off her back, and she saw the amusement in his bright blue eyes.

"I feel very adored," she said. Heathcliff danced around their feet, barking with joy. She reached down and gave his ears a good scratching, and then he darted off to patrol their yard.

She watched him go and glanced toward the house. "I wonder if Zelda will be as enthusiastic to see us."

Sully grabbed their bags from the back of Robbie's car, and they strode into the house. Zelda was sitting in the foyer. She was a gorgeous Russian Blue rescue cat that they acquired the year before when she appeared to be a stray in need of a home. She glanced at them, her green eyes unblinking, and then proceeded to lick her chest.

"Hello, sweetie." Lindsey bent down to pet her but Zelda turned away, striding out of the foyer and into the living room with her tail in the air.

"I can feel the love," she said. Her tone was dry and Sully laughed.

"It overwhelms," he agreed.

Lindsey went to the kitchen to put the kettle on. Sully shook Robbie's hand and said, "Thanks for the lift and for minding the pets."

"Anytime." Robbie slid onto a stool at the counter. Zelda, the traitor, crossed the room to rub her face against his shins. He glanced at Sully and Lindsey and smirked. "Told you so."

Sully rolled his eyes and kissed the top of Lindsey's head. "I plan to be home for dinner, but I'll let you know if I'll be late."

"Just be careful," she said. She hugged him tight. Maybe it was seeing Henry alive one minute and dead the next, but she hated that Sully was headed out onto the open water in a blizzard. Hated it.

"Don't make me come out there after you, Sailor Boy," Robbie said. His voice was teasing but the concern in his pale green gaze was genuine.

"I don't think the waterways are ready for that," Sully said. With a wave, he left them in the kitchen, letting Heathcliff in on his way out.

Heathcliff shook off his shaggy black coat in the foyer, sending snowflakes and water everywhere. Lindsey laughed. "I think he brought half of the yard in with him."

She went to grab a towel and said, "Mind the kettle?"

"Of course," Robbie agreed.

By the time Lindsey had dried off Heathcliff as best she could, Robbie had the tea steeping in the pot. Being British, he had insisted Lindsey learn to make tea the "proper" way—somehow a tea bag in the microwave just didn't cut it—and she had all the fixings for traditional tea for whenever Robbie stopped by.

She sank onto a stool while Heathcliff took his treat to his dog bed in front of the fireplace and hunkered down, his life now perfectly in order since his pack was back. Zelda stretched out on the hearth above him, and Lindsey got the feeling they were waiting to hear the story she was about to share with Robbie, which was silly, and yet, they both watched her with keen interest.

"Start at the beginning," Robbie said. He pushed a plate of cheese, fruit and crackers at her while he fixed their tea.

Lindsey realized she hadn't eaten since breakfast on the train, and now that it was early afternoon, she was famished.

She loaded up a cracker and took the cup that Robbie handed her. Snow, tea and a snack. All she needed was a book and a fire in the fireplace, and she'd be content. Except how could she be when someone had murdered Henry?

She swallowed her cracker and sipped her tea. Robbie sat on the stool beside her and waited. Lindsey took a breath and then told him about the train ride, starting with Lydia and Henry's altercation and ending with Henry being found dead in his compartment.

"So, you think this Lydia person murdered him?" Robbie asked. "That seems logical given their history."

"Too logical," Lindsey said.

"What do you mean?" Robbie asked. "It's a regular Occam's razor, isn't it?"

"You mean the theory that the simplest explanation is usually the right one?" Lindsey asked.

"Exactly," he said. "This Lydia person had motive and means, so why wouldn't it be her?"

"Because that's an oversimplification," Lindsey said. "What Occam's razor actually means is that extra evidence shouldn't be added when unnecessary. It's more about paring down information to find the truth more easily."

Robbie shook his head. "Isn't that the same thing? And doesn't that reinforce the theory that Lydia Armand—I really need to meet her—is guilty?"

"No, it actually means that if we take away all the anecdotal information about Lydia, which is extra information, then we are left without any real evidence that she murdered Henry."

"Hmm." Robbie sipped his tea and nibbled a cracker. "What about the others? His assistant Penny? Her paramour Kirk? Is there any indication that either of them killed Henry?"

"Not that I'm aware of," Lindsey said. She wished Robbie had met them all so he could have gotten a feeling for them. "Wait. I have the conference directory. It has pictures of Henry and Penny and maybe the others, although not Lydia because she went under a different name."

"Which in and of itself is suspect," Robbie said.

"You're not wrong," she agreed.

Lindsey hopped off her stool and crossed to her luggage in the foyer. Her laptop bag was hooked onto the handle of her carry-on, and she unzipped the pocket where she thought she'd packed the directory. A conference tote bag was in the pocket, and she frowned. She was certain she'd packed her tote into her carry-on. She took it out and felt a book inside.

Her heart started to hammer in her chest, and her breathing became shallow. It couldn't be. It was impossible.

"Everything all right, pet?" Robbie asked. "You look peaky, like you've seen a ghost."

"That depends upon whether books have ghosts," she said.

"Huh?" Robbie stood and crossed the room to her. "What's wrong?"

"Remember the book I told you about that went missing?" Lindsey asked.

"The Highsmith volume inscribed to Hitchcock?"

Lindsey nodded. She held up the tote bag. "I think this might be it."

"Go on, then," Robbie urged her.

Lindsey opened the bag and reached inside. Sure enough, it was the missing volume of *Strangers on a Train*.

CHAPTER
9

BRIAR CREEK
PUBLIC LIBRARY

I have to take this to Emma," Lindsey said. "Right away."

"Of course," Robbie agreed. Then he glanced at her. "Can I just see the inscription?"

"Robbie!"

"No, seriously, when will I ever get the chance to see such a thing?" he asked.

"All right, but be careful with it," Lindsey said. She held out the book and then took it back. "Are your hands clean?"

"Lindsey!"

"Fine, okay, here." She handed him the book.

Robbie opened it up to the title page. He read the inscription and said, "Wow."

"I know, it's like a slice of history." She glanced over his shoulder. Robbie flipped through the book, looking at the pages. He paused. There was writing in the margin of one. "What's this?"

Lindsey squinted. There were notes in the margins. It was a loopy handwriting. Hard to decipher.

"That doesn't match Highsmith's writing in the front," she said.

"No, but they read as if they're notes for . . ." He paused, studying the words.

"Notes for what?" Lindsey demanded.

"I might be mistaken, wouldn't be the first time, but I think these notes are Hitchcock's for writing the screenplay."

"No!" Lindsey cried. "That would make this book even more valuable. How did we not see these notes before?"

"You were too busy trying to hot potato it out of your possession, that's how," he said. "And it doesn't sound like your book restorer got much of a chance to peruse it either. You know, there was a huge blowout between Hitchcock and Raymond Chandler over the screenplay?"

"I didn't know," Lindsey said.

"Oh, yeah, real Hollywood 'you'll never work in this town again' sort of stuff," Robbie said. He looked delighted.

"Henry did give us the bum-rush out of there. Hitchcock's notes and Highsmith's inscription . . . I can't even imagine the value of this book," Lindsey said.

Robbie glanced away from the book and looked at her in wonder. "Hang on. Before we get carried away, let's check the handwriting. It could be the highlights of some random reader who decimates the value of the book with their scribbles."

Lindsey nodded. "You're right. We could be totally wrong."

Robbie took out his phone and did a quick search of images of Alfred Hitchcock's handwriting. Lindsey put the book down on the counter, and Robbie put his phone beside it, enlarging the best sample he'd found.

"I'm no expert, but I'd say that's a match," he said.

Lindsey picked out individual letters. The *d*'s were the same, the *t*'s were identical, and the *i*'s were dotted exactly alike.

"It's either a very good forgery or it's authentic," she said. "I wish Brooklyn Wainwright was here. I'd love her opinion."

"You could email her," he suggested.

"I suppose, but it's not the same," Lindsey said. "Also, I feel like we'd have more leverage with questioning people if she was here."

"Because you'd have an expert on hand?" he asked.

"Something like that," she said. She did not mention that Brooklyn had been involved in some high-profile murder investigations and Lindsey would be more than happy to hand that off to her as well.

Zelda was purring and rubbing her face on Robbie's pant leg. Lindsey reached down to stroke her head, and Zelda turned and walked away. Lindsey sighed and shook her head.

"How long do you think she's going to be annoyed with me?" she asked.

"Hard to say since she's a cat," Robbie said. "Are they known for holding grudges?"

"Cold shoulders," Lindsey said. "I've heard they're very good at those."

"She's master level, for sure," he agreed. He glanced back at the book and put his phone away. "Drink your tea, then. If we're going to the inn to see Emma, we should do it quickly before the storm gets worse."

The drive to the inn was treacherous, but since Robbie had an all-wheel drive SUV-truck hybrid, they managed it just fine. All of the lights were on at the inn, and smoke was pluming out of the chimney. Lindsey had taken the precaution to wrap the book back in its tote bag and seal both items in a thick plastic bag. She didn't want to be responsible for anything happening to it.

The main entrance to the inn was a large, marble-floored lobby with a check-in desk on one side and a fireplace with comfy chairs in front of it on the other. Michelle Brioni, the owner, was seated behind the desk. She glanced up at the sound of the door opening and said, "I'm sorry, we're not taking—oh, Lindsey, Robbie, never mind. I know you two don't need rooms. But what are you doing here and out in this weather?"

"Hi, Michelle," Lindsey said. "We're here to see Emma. Also, I was sorry to hear about the wedding. That had to be insanely stressful."

Michelle cringed. "What a disaster. Honestly, I don't know who was more revolting, the groom or the maid of honor." She leaned over the desk and said, "The bride got a nice shot off the groom's particulars, if you know what I mean, and I say good for her."

Lindsey nodded while Robbie looked pained. "I had no idea you were so bloodthirsty, Michelle. Next audition for the community theater, I'm recommending you for a fight scene."

Michelle laughed. She was in her midfifties, her graying hair highlighted with blond streaks, and while her face showed her years with fine lines around her nose and mouth, she had a sparkle in her eyes and a spring in her step that time could not diminish. It had been a hard-fought battle to keep that sparkle and spring.

Three years ago, Michelle's husband and business partner had run off to Costa Rica with the inn's cook to live out his days as a beach bum. Michelle had been gutted. No one had seen it coming, least of all Michelle. Depressed, she'd considered selling the place, but she loved the inn, it was also her home, and she decided to stay. The community had rallied around her, helping her find a new cook and bolstering her business by recommending it to any and all tourists who passed through.

After a year, Michelle decided that she could handle the business on her own. Not only could she handle it, she could make enough money to survive and thrive. She'd hosted a good riddance party at the inn the night her divorce had come through and had seemed to turn a corner after that. Lindsey knew Michelle was an audio book listener, as she'd said she enjoyed listening to books while working around the inn. Lindsey had gotten her hooked on several long-running series that were downloadable through the library, their mutual favorite being the Cork O'Connor series by William Kent Krueger.

"Emma is in the café," Michelle said. "She's interviewing the passengers, none of whom want to be here. I really hope they don't blast the inn with bad reviews just because of the circumstances."

"If they do, we'll just add a comment outing them as a suspect in a murder investigation," Robbie said. "That'll shut them up."

"Now who's the bloodthirsty one?" Michelle asked with a grin.

"How many people from the train are staying here?" Lindsey asked.

"Thirty-two," Michelle answered. "A full house, luckily a few of them agreed to share rooms."

"Do tell." Robbie leaned on the counter, resting his chin in his hand.

Michelle leaned forward and ruffled his reddish blond hair. "Scamp," she said, but her voice was warm with affection. "There are several married couples in the group."

"That disappoints," Robbie said.

Lindsey gave him a quelling look. "Do you think Emma would mind if we interrupted her?"

"Yes, but only because that's how Emma is," Michelle said. "She didn't ask not to be disturbed and she's got her right-hand man, Officer Kirkland, in there with her, so she could probably step out for a moment."

"It is important," Lindsey said.

Michelle's eyebrows rose. "Go straight down the hall-way, and it's the last room on your left. If Emma isn't happy to see you, I was not the one who directed you to her, capisce?"

"We never saw you," Lindsey said.

Michelle winked. "Carry on."

Lindsey and Robbie left the lobby. The hallway was empty. There was no noise coming from any of the guests in the building, and she wondered if they were all in their rooms, napping, watching the snow or thinking up lies to get out of being caught for murder.

She shook her head. She was getting a bit ahead of herself. First things first, she needed to give Emma the book. The way it appeared in her bag, she almost felt as if she were starring in a horror movie and the book was possessed by a spirit that had latched on to her. Nope, nope, nope. It was official. There was way too much Hitchcock happening in her head.

And yet, how could the book have ended up in her bag unless someone—the killer?—planted it there? A shiver rippled up Lindsey's spine. She told herself it was the cold even though the inn was perfectly warm and cozy.

"All right, Linds?" Robbie asked. He gave her a side-eye.

"I'm fine," she said.

He patted her shoulder. "The book is not possessed by evil spirits. It's not following you. Whoever murdered Henry likely tucked it into your bag when you weren't looking so that they could retrieve it later, except Henry's body was discovered and their plan went all to heck."

"That's exactly what I was thinking," Lindsey said. "I think if we could trace the book's whereabouts from the conference to the train to my bag, we'd find our killer."

They reached the door. Officer Kirkland was standing outside, doing a fine impression of a brick wall. At the sight of Lindsey and Robbie approaching, he sighed audibly.

"For the record, we had no intention of coming here this afternoon," Robbie said.

"And yet, here you are," Kirkland said. He had one eyebrow raised in doubt.

"I have something important to give to Emma," Lindsey said.

"It's not a good time," Kirkland said. "She's talking to the train passengers right now."

"I know, and I hate to interrupt, but I think it might have something to do with the murder," Lindsey said. She held up the plastic bag she carried so he could see she actually had brought something with her.

Kirkland straightened up as he studied the item in her hands. "Is it the murder weapon?"

"No," Lindsey said. Then she added, "At least, I don't think so."

She couldn't imagine how the book could have been used to murder someone. If they'd hit Henry with it, it would be damaged. Same thing if they'd wrestled for it.

"Are you sure it can't wait?" he asked. "If I interrupt her, the chief might be . . ." His voice trailed off as if he didn't want to commit to words whatever he was thinking.

"It's all right, mate, we're two of her nearest and dearest, we know how she can be," Robbie said. "But trust us, she'll want to know about this."

"Fine." Kirkland turned away from them and knocked on the door before opening it and poking his head in. "Chief, there's someone out here to speak with you."

"Tell them I'm busy," Emma called out.

Robbie poked his head in the opening beside Kirkland. "Surprise!"

"Robbie, what are you doing here?" Emma cried.

"Is that Robbie Vine, the actor?" a voice from inside the room asked. "Oh my God, it is! Can I take a picture with you?"

"Oh, for—" The rest of Emma's rant was muffled, but Lindsey suspected she knew what the chief was saying. She heard Emma stride toward the door, and she started when Emma barked, "Out! Get out!"

Both Robbie and Kirkland jumped back from the door just in time as Emma came through like her own personal storm front.

"Lindsey!" Emma stared at her as if she couldn't believe she was a participant in this disruption of her investigation.

"I know, I know," Lindsey said. "I'm sorry, but I found something, and Robbie came with me because I don't have a car, because Sully took the truck so he could get to the pier to take last-minute supplies to the islanders."

"All right, fine, what did you find?" Emma asked.

"I was looking for the conference program in my laptop bag, when I found this." She held out the plastic bag containing the tote bag and the book.

Emma took it and turned it over in her hands. "What is it?"

"A very rare, very valuable book that I think might be the reason why Henry Standish was murdered," Lindsey said.

"The book!" a voice cried from the open door. "You found the book?"

They all turned to see Penny Minton standing in the doorway. Her eyes were wide behind her glasses, and she looked shocked to see the bundle in Emma's hands.

Emma looked from Lindsey to Penny and then down at the book. "Tell me about the book."

"I found it under my seat at the conference," Lindsey said. "It's a first edition volume of the Patricia Highsmith novel *Strangers on a Train*, in excellent condition and in-scribed to Alfred Hitchcock. The book restorer who was at the conference believed it was very valuable, and that's be-fore Robbie and I found notes from Hitchcock himself in the margins."

Emma tucked the plastic bag under her arm while she pulled on a pair of blue latex gloves that she had in her pocket. She carefully opened the plastic and took out the tote bag. The conference logo was on it, and Lindsey won-dered if it was the same one she'd found the book in ori-ginally.

Kirkland pulled on his gloves as well and held the bag open so that Emma could remove the novel. She turned it over in her hands and then opened the cover and studied the title page.

"Has the inscription or the signature been authenticated?" she asked.

"It was," Penny answered. "The item was supposed to be in the silent auction on the opening night of the conference, but the anonymous donor removed it at the last minute."

"No explanation?" Emma asked.

Penny shook her head. "It was believed that they just changed their mind. It happens sometimes. People get very attached to their things."

"So it was removed from the auction and then you found it under your chair?" Emma asked Lindsey. "So, it was stolen from the donor?"

"Potentially," Lindsey agreed. "When I found it, I turned it over to Henry."

"Who turned it over to me," Penny said.

There was a shuffling sound, and Lindsey noticed that most of the people who'd been at the conference who'd also been on the train were now crowding the doorway, trying to listen to the conversation.

"Then what happened to it?" Emma asked.

"I was supposed to find out who it belonged to," Penny said. "But since the donor for the auction was anonymous, I couldn't. When I told Henry, he took it back and said he would hang on to it for safekeeping until we got back to the office, where he had more comprehensive donation records."

Emma closed the book and put it back in the tote bag, which she returned to the plastic bag. She handed it to Kirkland. "Let's get this to the state crime lab and see if they can find any clues in it."

"Ah!" Lydia Armand cried as she pushed her way out of the room. "You can't do that."

"Excuse me?" Emma asked.

"That is an incredibly rare artifact, and if they mistreat it, it could be damaged beyond repair," Lydia said.

"She's right," Lindsey said. "If they dusted it for fingerprints or took it apart to examine the binding, its archival quality would be compromised."

Emma sent Lindsey a reproving look. "Are you saying a book is more important than a dead man?"

"No, of course not," Lindsey said. "It's just there are ways to examine it that won't damage it. If you'd like, I could reach out to the university and see if I can get an expert to work with the crime lab so that no harm is done to the volume." She paused and then added, "Henry would want that."

Emma frowned. "All right." She turned to Kirkland. "Take it to the station and lock it up in the vault until Lindsey has someone willing to work with the crime lab." She glanced at Lindsey and added, "You have twenty-four hours, and then I'm going ahead."

"Twenty-four hours after the storm passes," Lindsey amended. "There's no way I can get anyone out here during this." She gestured out the window. The blizzard was now looking like a full whiteout, and she felt a pang of fear that Sully was out on the open water. She took a steadying breath. No one knew the islands better, and he wasn't a fool. He wouldn't take any unnecessary risks.

"Fine, but not one minute more," Emma agreed.

Lindsey didn't think she imagined the collective sigh of relief that the group of archivists shared.

"That's all great and good," Lydia said. "But I have a question."

"Okay," Emma said.

Lydia ignored her and set her gaze on Lindsey. Her eyes narrowed in suspicion and she asked, "Why you?"

"What do you mean?" Lindsey replied.

"Of all the people on the train last night, why did the missing book end up in *your* luggage?"

CHAPTER

10

BRIAR CREEK
PUBLIC LIBRARY

Lindsey was keenly aware that all eyes were on her. She felt her face get warm, as she disliked being the center of attention. She tipped her chin up and met Lydia's gaze.

"Honestly, I have no idea," she said. "Which is why I brought the book straight to the police."

She felt the tension drop immediately. Of course, the fact that she'd brought it to Emma right away made her look innocent. *Innocent?* Was Lydia actually insinuating that she had something to do with Henry's murder? She frowned. She had thought Lydia considered her an equal when they spoke on the train. She wondered why Lydia seemed to be turning on her now.

"Which was exactly the right thing to do," Emma said. "Just as I expect that all of you will come to me if you remember anything or think of anything that feels relevant or important to the case. The sooner we get this sorted, the sooner you can all leave."

"I still say you can't keep us here," Andrew said. "We have homes and families we need to get to."

"Well, since the rail service has shut down because of ice on the tracks, you can be grateful that you're here and not with the other passengers, who are now hunkered down in Union Station in New Haven awaiting improved conditions," Emma said. She waited a beat and added, "You're welcome."

"What happens next?" Penny asked.

"I'll be calling each of you in for an individual interview, but in the meantime, you can go to your assigned rooms and stay there," Emma said. "When it's your turn, one of my officers will collect you and escort you here. Feel free to make use of the inn's facilities, but do not under any circumstances leave the premises."

"And if we do?" asked one of the passengers, a middle-aged man wearing an overly tight suit, whom Lindsey didn't know.

"You'll be arrested, and I think you'll find the accommodations at our local jail much less desirable than your own room at a comfortable inn," Emma said cheerfully.

The group exited the room, grumbling and mumbling, in a meandering line out the door to the stairs that led to the upper floors.

"Come on in," Emma said. "I have questions. Many questions."

Kirkland took the book, departing for the police station before the weather made it impossible. Emma stepped aside, and Lindsey and Robbie entered the room. The smell of roses overwhelmed, and Lindsey felt her nose twitch. She had a history with roses, which did not make them her favorite flower. She glanced around the space. It had obviously been the room where the bride and groom had planned to exchange vows.

Folding chairs were set up in orderly rows with the chairs on the end of the aisle festooned with roses wrapped in pine boughs and tied together with a silver ribbon. At the front of the room was a large silver arch decorated with more of the roses, pine boughs and silver ribbon. The sight of the wilting flowers made Lindsey sad. A bride had planned a beautiful day to celebrate her love, and instead it had ended in betrayal and dead flowers.

"I know," Emma said. "I hate being in here, but it was the only room with enough chairs to accommodate all of our . . . guests."

"You didn't really arrest the bride, did you?" Lindsey asked.

"Mercifully, no," Emma said. "The groom and the maid of honor opted not to press charges."

"Big of them," Robbie said. His sarcasm was as thick as the scent of the roses. Emma grunted in agreement. Lindsey suspected that even if they had pressed charges, Emma would have released the bride on her own recognizance.

Emma gestured for them to sit. Lindsey sat in the last

row of chairs, while Emma and Robbie took seats in the row in front of her and turned them around so that they were facing her.

"I know you've been thinking this over, so you won't be surprised when I ask. At what point was your bag left unattended on the train?" Emma asked. "Because I'm assuming that whoever put that book into your bag had to have done it on the train, as you would have noticed before you checked out of the hotel."

"Yes, I would have," Lindsey agreed. "And I know for a fact that they didn't put it in there before last night because Sully and I watched the movie version of *Strangers on a Train* on my laptop."

"Interesting choice," Robbie said. "A bit on the nose, wasn't it?"

"Sully had never seen the movie or read the book," Lindsey said.

"Blasphemy!" Robbie said. Emma shot him a quelling look, and he leaned back in his chair while miming zipping his lips closed.

"That means that the only time they could have put the book in my bag was when we were waiting to enter Henry's compartment," Lindsey said. "We were all in the passageway, and our door was open. Anyone could have accessed our room, and in the chaos we didn't notice. We had breakfast with Andrew Shields and Lydia Armand, but we returned to our car ahead of them."

"That accounts for those two, then," Robbie said.

"Not really," Emma said. "We have no evidence that it's only one person who participated in Henry's death. It sounds like he stacked up enemies like firewood. There could have been more than one person involved."

"That would make sense," Lindsey said.

"Tell me what you know about the relationships of the people closest to Standish," Emma said.

"I don't know much," Lindsey said. "I only knew Henry in a professional capacity and just in passing, and that was back when I was an archivist at the Beinecke Rare Book and Manuscript Library at Yale University."

The windowpane rattled against a sudden gust of wind, and she glanced outside. The snow was even thicker and more alarming than it had been when she and Robbie arrived. They were close to a full-on whiteout situation. She wondered if the weather was as bad on the water or if the salt of the sea made visibility better. She reached into her bag and took out her phone. There were no messages from Sully, and she didn't want to bother him while he was working.

"He'll be all right," Emma said. "No one knows the islands better than Sully."

Lindsey flashed her a smile of appreciation. She knew Emma was right and, yet, the nagging feeling in her gut persisted.

"Em's right. He's the only person I know who's more at home on water than on land," Robbie said. "But we can't stay much longer or we won't be able to leave, and I don't think your pets would appreciate that."

"Yes, of course." Lindsey shook her head to adjust her focus. She turned to Emma and started telling her every detail she could remember about finding the book and her observations of Henry and Penny. She then told her about the altercation between Henry and Lydia on the train and between Henry and Kirk after Henry humiliated Penny. Emma's eyebrows rose but she said nothing.

"Of course you already know about how we found Henry this morning," Lindsey said. "Our car attendant Patrick was the only one to enter the roomette, and he declared Henry dead when he checked his vitals and found nothing, but honestly, it was obvious to all of us that Henry had died."

"How was it obvious?" Emma asked.

Lindsey swallowed and said, "You saw him. His neck was off, you know? It was bent at an unnatural angle, and his eyes were open and he was staring vacantly at us. We just . . . knew."

Emma reached forward and patted Lindsey's arm. "I'm sorry you had to see that. It was rough, even for me."

"Yeah, but I had Sully . . ." Lindsey hopped up from her seat. "I have to go. I can't explain it, but something's wrong."

"What?" Emma asked.

"I don't know," Lindsey admitted. "Maybe I'm just stressed by what happened to Henry, but I need to get to the pier right away."

"The pier?" Robbie glanced at her face and stood up. "I'll take you."

Emma studied Lindsey. "I have to stay here and interview these people, but I want you to call me as soon as Sully gets in or you make contact with him."

"Will do." Lindsey nodded as she walked to the door. Her skin itched, everything felt out of whack, and if she hadn't had Robbie to drive her to the pier, she would have run there herself.

"Be careful," Emma said to Robbie. "I mean it."

"Of course, love," he agreed. He kissed her quick and hurried to catch up to Lindsey, who was already striding down the hallway to the lobby of the inn.

Michelle glanced at them from the front desk. She was frowning. "You're not going back out in that, are you?"

"Yes, we are," Lindsey said. Her voice was defiant as if she expected Michelle to stop her. Michelle blinked and Robbie sent her a sympathetic look. Lindsey realized she sounded too fierce for the situation. "Sorry, I'm just . . . I have to go."

Michelle studied her and then she nodded. "Wait here for one second." She disappeared into the office behind her and came right back out, carrying two thick gray wool blankets and a flashlight. "Just in case you get into trouble out there."

"Thanks, Michelle," Lindsey said. She grabbed the items, and when Robbie opened the door, they dashed out into the brutal wind and biting cold. The snow was so sharp it pricked the exposed skin of their faces like a thousand needles.

Robbie pressed the fob for his car, and the lights flashed as the doors unlocked. They jumped inside, and Lindsey turned to look at him. "You don't have to come. You could just loan me your car."

He looked at her as if she were daft. "Of course I do. Sully's my best mate, and I know he'd do the same for me."

He turned the car on, and they buckled up while the windshield wipers tried to clear the glass of snow and ice. With the headlights on, they could just make out the road. Robbie was forced to drive excruciatingly slowly back into the center of town.

The plows hadn't gotten to the side roads yet, and the inn sat at the end of a very long, winding, narrow one. A ditch ran along the passenger side, and Lindsey knew if Robbie veered too far to the right, they'd be stuck in the trench until someone came to pull them out. That was not happening. Not on her watch.

"Mailbox on your right," she said.

"Got it," Robbie replied. He swerved slightly to the left. They inched their way up the road, avoiding fire hydrants, fences and trash cans.

Finally, at the crest of the hill, they came to the main road, which looked as if it had been plowed at the beginning of the storm. The asphalt was swiftly being covered up again, but the tracks were there, and they could see them well enough to follow.

"Bloody hell, this is the worst storm I've ever been in," Robbie said.

Lindsey glanced out the window where she knew the

bay was. She couldn't see it through the veil of pelting snow, but she knew Sully was out there somewhere.

Robbie glanced at her and followed her line of sight before refocusing on the road. "He's probably already headed back to the pier. In fact, I'll bet you a hot cup of chowder at the Blue Anchor that he's already back."

"No," Lindsey said. "He would have texted me."

"Maybe he's just warming up his fingers," Robbie said. He nudged her with his elbow. "Give him a call. You're working yourself into a state, and it might be for nothing."

Lindsey nodded. She felt as if her insides had been scooped out and her body cavity packed with snow. That's how frozen she felt in her core. Her fingers were shaking, not from the cold, as she took out her phone and chose Sully out of her contacts. His phone rang eight times and then it switched over to voice mail. She didn't leave a message, choosing to end the call instead.

"No answer," she said.

"Right, then," Robbie said. "It's likely he can't hear his phone ringing over the boat engine or some such. Nothing to worry about."

He pressed the accelerator down, increasing their speed, and Lindsey knew that despite his words he was as worried as she was.

They arrived at the pier, parking in the lot outside the Blue Anchor restaurant, which was clearly closed, as all the lights were off. Sully's sister, Mary, owned the restaurant with her husband, Ian Murphy, who also shared ownership in the water taxi and tour business with Sully.

Lindsey suspected they were home with their baby girl, riding out the storm like anyone with an ounce of sense. The wind whipped at their scarves and coats as she and Robbie walked down the pier to Sully's office. The lights were on, giving Lindsey a flicker of hope that Sully had returned.

Robbie reached the door first and yanked it open. Ronnie, who ran the office for Sully and Ian, was seated at her desk, staring at the radio she used to communicate with the boats as if willing it to make some noise. When she glanced up at Lindsey, there was no disguising the worry in her eyes.

In her mid eighties and a lifelong resident of Briar Creek, Ronnie, with her cranberry-colored hair and big, knobby plastic jewelry circa the early nineteen seventies, had seen her share of tragedy hit the small village. The expression on her face was that of a person bracing for the worst.

"Ronnie, what's happening?" Lindsey asked. "Where's Sully?"

"I'm sorry, doll," Ronnie said. She raised her hands in the air in defeat. "I have no idea. He was supposed to radio in when he arrived at Bell Island, it was his first stop, but he never did."

"You mean he never even made it to his parents' house?" Lindsey asked. She felt her heart thump in her chest. This was bad, so bad.

"What can we do?" Robbie asked.

Ronnie shook her head. "Ian's out there, looking for him."

"Oh no, not Ian, too." Lindsey put her fingers to her lips.

"Ian's fine," Ronnie said. "He's on the phone with Mary, who's standing out on the pier. She wouldn't let him go unless he promised to stay on the phone the entire time."

"Smart," Lindsey said. Why hadn't she thought of that? She felt like she might be sick.

The radio crackled, and Ian's voice came on. "Ronnie, you there?"

Ronnie snatched up the mouthpiece. "Yes, I'm here. Did you find Sully?"

There was a pause. The wind whistled in the background, and the radio hissed. Lindsey dug her fingers into her palms until her nails made dents in her skin. The pain kept her present.

"I didn't find him," Ian said. His voice was heavy, and it cracked with emotion when he continued, "It's bad, Ronnie. I found his boat, but he wasn't on it."

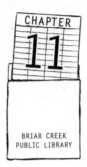

CHAPTER

11

BRIAR CREEK
PUBLIC LIBRARY

L indsey didn't wait to hear any more. She banged out of the office and ran toward the end of the pier. Under the bright spotlight, she saw a lone figure standing there. The hood of her heavy coat was up, and she wore thick-soled boots and snow pants. She was dressed for this weather, and Lindsey knew that if Mary had to stand there all night, looking for her husband and her brother, she would.

"Mary!" Lindsey cried as she ran down the pier, through the patches of yellow lamplight that illuminated the pier in the thick curtain of falling snow.

Mary whirled around. "Lindsey!" And then into the phone she said, "Yes, she's here with me. Yes, I'll tell her. I can see you. Come back with the boat and we'll decide what to do next."

She ended the call and looked at Lindsey. "That was Ian, he's found—"

"Sully's boat, I know," Lindsey said. "I was in the office when he called in to Ronnie."

Mary opened her arms and Lindsey stepped in, holding on to her sister-in-law as if she were an anchor in a turbulent sea. She did not believe that Sully was lost to her. She couldn't believe it. She wouldn't believe it.

"There's Ian!" Robbie shouted over the wind as he joined them. He pointed at a light bobbing on the water coming toward the pier. "I'm going down to help him tie up. Wait here."

Mary and Lindsey waited a beat, and then Lindsey stepped away from her sister-in-law and said, "I'm going down, too."

"Copy that," Mary said.

They wound their way down the stairs to the dock below. The wind tore at their clothes, and it was so bitterly cold it actually felt like any exposed skin was being frozen. Lindsey wrapped her scarf about her face and tightened her hood around her head.

Robbie caught the rope that Ian tossed him, and he knelt on the dock to tie it down. Sully's boat was behind Ian's and pulling against the tow rope. The engine was off and it bobbed on the white-capped water as if trying to break free to go back and look for its captain.

Lindsey and Mary hurried forward to help, and as soon as Sully's boat was close enough, they grabbed it, pulling it in until it was adjacent to the dock, nestled up against the fat rubber tires that protected it from damage, right behind Ian's. Mary climbed aboard and threw one of the tie ropes to Lindsey. She crouched down beside the metal cleat, but when she went to loop the rope around it, there was already a hank of rope there.

Her fingers were stiff from the cold even with her gloves on, and trying to take the remainder of the rope off took some effort. She tossed the piece aside and looped the tie in a figure eight the way Sully had taught her. Mary had hopped off the boat and was securing the other rope. Once the craft was stable, Lindsey climbed aboard, looking for something, anything, that would tell her what might have happened to her husband.

There was nothing. The supplies he'd been bringing to the islanders were still boxed in their big plastic bins in the back of the boat. There was no sign of a struggle, not like with Henry, where his entire train compartment had been in disarray. Other than snow, there was no water in the bottom of the boat, so he hadn't been caught in anything so rough that it might have washed him overboard. In fact, as she studied the interior of Sully's boat, it looked remarkably untouched.

Lindsey assumed that if he'd hit rough weather, the boat would be swamped, the supplies dumped overboard, and his emergency flare sent up. She'd heard no report of a flare being spotted. She ducked down behind the windshield and checked Sully's emergency supply bin. Everything in it, including the flare gun, was in perfect order. She moved to the captain's chair and studied the console. She picked up the radio and pressed the button.

"Ronnie, can you hear me?" she asked.

"Lindsey! What's happening?" Ronnie's voice came back loud and clear. "Did you find Sully?"

"No, I'm standing in his boat," she said. "I wanted to test the radio. We're all coming up."

"Roger that," Ronnie said. "I'll make coffee."

Lindsey looked back at the dock, where Robbie, Mary and Ian were watching her. What she could see of their faces behind the hats, hoods and scarves was grim. Their eyes were all shadowed with fear, and Lindsey knew they were worried that somehow Sully had been swept out to sea. But she didn't see any evidence of that. She went to climb out, when an object on the floor of the boat caught her eye.

It glowed and she dropped to her knees to grab it. It was Sully's phone. She recognized it right away, as the display screen was a picture of them, ironically in a snowstorm, on their wedding day. It was lit with notifications of all the calls and texts he'd received over the past few hours, including hers. Lindsey pocketed the phone, not wanting to risk dropping it in the water when she jumped from the boat to the dock.

This was more evidence that something bad had happened to Sully. Lindsey felt the fear and worry bloom in the pit of her stomach, but then she realized that she didn't believe it. Lindsey refused to sink into despair. The fear was a reaction to an unexplained circumstance. She tamped down her panic and tried to look at the situation through a logical lens. Given everything she'd seen—the remnants of rope on the cleats, the supplies still on board, the boat dry and not swamped in water—she believed that something had happened to Sully before he left the dock on his boat.

She hurried to Ian and shouted over the wind, "Where did you find his boat? Was it out around the islands?"

"No, I spotted it from the pier in the shallow water of the bay." Ian raised his voice. "According to Ronnie, he never called in. I don't think he made it out to the islands."

Her panic began to froth and churn inside her again. Lindsey shook it off. She had no time for hysterics. She pointed up with her right hand at the others, and they nodded, correctly interpreting the signal that they should all go up to the pier.

They climbed the steps and hurried back to the warm office, where Ronnie waited. The wind and snow chased them inside, and Ian closed the door behind them, shutting the blizzard out. Ronnie was in the midst of making the pot of coffee as they stomped the snow off their boots and unwound their scarves. They shed their coats and rubbed their hands together, trying to chase the cold out of their fingers.

Ronnie pressed the brew button and then turned to face them all. Much like the others, her expression was tight, her eyes shadowed with fear. "Now what do we do?" she asked. "Should I call the Coast Guard?"

"Emma is on it," Robbie said. "I called her right before

I joined you lot on the pier. She knows we found Sully's boat without him in it. I thought we'd have a better chance of getting the Coast Guard involved if it came from an official channel."

"Good thinking," Lindsey said. She waited a beat and added, "But I don't think Sully was ever on that boat."

"What? How do you know?" Mary asked.

"I don't know for sure, but there are a couple of things that indicate to me that he never got on it. First, Ian found the boat drifting in the shallows. If Sully had made it to the islands, the boat wouldn't have been so close to the shore. Second, when we went to tie it up, there was a bit of rope still on the cleat on the dock," Lindsey said. "I had to take that remainder off before I could secure Sully's boat." She glanced at Mary. "Did you find the same thing on yours?"

Mary frowned. "Yes. There was a short length of rope still wrapped around it. I assumed Sully wasn't able to get it untied with the frigid temperatures and cut it."

Lindsey glanced at Ian. "Does that seem likely?"

Ian pursed his lips while he considered. "No, Sully's gotten the boat untied in worse weather than this, and he's never had to cut the ropes."

"But both ropes were cut," Lindsey said. "If it wasn't Sully, that means someone else did it. And lastly, I found his phone on the floor of the boat. Why would he have taken it out of his pocket?"

"To check the weather?" Mary asked.

"I think he could see the weather just fine," Ian countered.

"I think someone cut his boat loose and they grabbed him," Lindsey said. Her voice cracked when she said it, and she cleared her throat and added, "And I think they threw his phone into his boat so that if we tracked him, it would show him out on the water."

"But why?" Robbie asked the obvious question. "Why would someone do that?"

Lindsey started to pace while Ian and Mary sat on the small love seat and Robbie took one of the armchairs. "I don't know, but I feel positive that the ropes were cut on the boat just after Sully loaded his supplies, and then the person pushed the boat free. They wanted it gone, probably so we wouldn't look for Sully too soon."

"Who would do this? And where do they have Sully?" Mary's voice trembled when she asked, "I mean, do you think they would have knocked him out and thrown him off the pier to die of hypothermia?"

Ian put his arm around his wife and pulled her close. The coffeepot beeped, and Ronnie grabbed some mugs from the shelf and put them on the small glass coffee table. She then brought the coffeepot over and started filling the mugs and handing them out. She'd brought sugar and a small carton of creamer as well, but Lindsey wanted hers black. She needed all the heat and bitterness to wake her up and clear her head.

"No, I don't think someone would go to all that trouble just to murder him." Lindsey took a sip and then shook her head. "They didn't harm him, because they need him for something. I just have no idea what."

Ian squeezed his temples. "I think I'm having an aneurysm. Why would someone do that to Sully? The man literally doesn't have any enemies. And if they did grab him so they could steal his boat or the supplies, why weren't they in the boat when I found it?"

"They didn't want the boat," Lindsey said. She glanced at Robbie, who was cupping his mug, letting the heat warm his hands as he mentally sifted through everything she said.

"A distraction?" Robbie hypothesized. He lifted one hand from the mug and snapped the fingers. "They didn't want to kill Sully. They wanted to use him as a distraction to get everyone looking away from the murder of Henry Standish. And by throwing his phone into the boat, as you said, if someone tried to track Sully using his phone, it would merely lead them to his boat, which they probably hoped had gotten lost amid the islands and would take ages to get to."

He met Lindsey's gaze and she nodded, letting him know she'd come to the same conclusion.

"Then how do we find Sully now?" Mary asked.

Lindsey deflated. "That I don't know."

"We need to loop in Emma," Robbie said. "If their plan really is to get law enforcement to look away from their current investigation, then she has to show a visible effort in looking for Sully to make them think it's working. That's the best shot we have of making them slip up."

Lindsey glanced outside. "The blizzard complicates things. Even if Emma wants to start looking for him, I don't think she's going to be able to leave the inn anytime soon."

They all glanced out the window. The wind was whipping the snow into massive drifts even on the pier. In fact, the snow was pushing up against the side of the office, and Lindsey doubted they'd be able to leave if they didn't go now.

"We'd better go," Ian said, clearly coming to the same conclusion. "Mary and I came to check on the restaurant. Beth and Aidan are watching Josie for us, but if we're going to pick her up, we'd better leave."

Ian and Mary downed their coffee, thanking Ronnie, who nodded. "Be careful out there."

"Can I give you a lift, Ronnie?" Ian asked. "I have my truck. I don't think your sedan can handle this much snow. In fact, it's probably buried."

"I can take her," Robbie said. He stood up and began to pull on his jacket and gloves. "My SUV can handle the snow, and I'm going right by her place on my way to drop off Lindsey."

"That works," Ronnie said. "I'll come back and get my car tomorrow." She glanced around the office. "I don't expect we'll be open. I'll forward the calls for the water taxi to my home number."

"Call me if you hear anything from Sully," Mary said. She hugged Lindsey, who said, "I will. I promise. But don't worry. He's all right. I know it."

Mary gave her a look that said louder than words that she hoped what Lindsey said was true. She and Ian ducked out into the cold, disappearing into the curtain of snow that continued to fall.

Ronnie collected the mugs and took them into the break room in the back of the office. Then she shut off the coffeepot and powered down her computer. She forwarded the landline to her home number and began to pull on her coat, hat and gloves. She glanced at Lindsey and asked, "The people on the island who were expecting deliveries will probably be calling anytime now. What should I tell them?"

Lindsey said, "The truth. That Sully couldn't make it but he'll be there as soon as he can."

Ronnie snorted. "Nice and vague. What about his parents? He was supposed to stop there first. I'm sure they're wondering what's happened to him by now."

They moved to the door. Ronnie snapped off the lights, leaving them standing in the glow of the night-light that came on when all the other lights were off.

"I'll call them when I get home," Lindsey said. She tugged on her gloves and fastened her coat. "I'll let them know what's happening."

Ronnie nodded, looking relieved that she wasn't going to have to be the bearer of bad news. She squinted at Lindsey and asked, "Do you really believe he's all right?"

"I do," Lindsey said. She was absolutely certain that he was okay right now. "I just don't know how much longer he'll remain so."

On that somber note, the three of them stepped out into the blizzard, disappearing into the whiteout as completely as if they'd been erased.

\* \* \*

Robbie dropped Ronnie off first, making certain she got inside and had power before he got back onto the road, what they could see of it, and turned toward Lindsey's home. The plows were out, moving slowly along the road, creating huge drifts on the curb as they tried to stay ahead of the storm.

"How long is it supposed to snow?" Lindsey asked.

"All night," Robbie said. "The front should move out to sea by morning."

Lindsey glanced at her phone. Morning was a long way away. Robbie pulled up to her house. They'd left a light on, so she knew she had power.

"What are you going to do now?" he asked.

"I'm going to call Emma and tell her what we suspect," she said.

"I can do that for you," he offered. "I'm headed back to the inn. Her police cruiser can't handle this weather, and even if she plans to spend the night there to keep watch on the suspects, I don't want her stuck there without an exit strategy."

"You're a good boyfriend," Lindsey said. He smiled. "Then I guess I'm going to call Sully's parents and let them know what's happening."

"That's a tough call to make," Robbie said.

"If it was me, I'd want to know," she said.

"True." He patted her shoulder. "We'll find him and he'll be all right."

Lindsey gave him a fleeting smile and then said, "Be careful and stay in touch."

"You as well," he said. "Do not even think about going out in this without proper transportation. Promise me."

"I promise," she said. She opened her door and stepped back out into the biting wind and snow. The headlights of Robbie's car illuminated the way until the motion-sensitive light by the front door snapped on. Lindsey took out her keys and unlocked the door, pulling it open and bracing herself for Heathcliff's exuberant greeting.

She turned and waved to Robbie and watched as he slowly backed his car down the driveway and turned onto the road. She was standing in the doorway but Heathcliff didn't appear. She let the door swing shut.

"Heathcliff!" she cried. She heard a low *woof* sound from down the hallway. She'd left the lights on in the living room, and a quick glance showed nothing amiss in the house. She walked down the hallway from where the noise had come.

Their cozy cape house had three bedrooms, the main one, which she shared with Sully, and then two others, which they'd made into a guest room and a home office. She followed the sound of Heathcliff's huffing noises into the office. She switched on the light by the door, and the overhead lamp snapped on, illuminating the room. Zelda was sprawled across the top of the desk while Heathcliff was on his dog bed in the corner.

"Hey, buddy," Lindsey said. "No hello? Are you feeling all right?"

She crossed the room and noticed that he had something on his bed. She reached down and pulled it out from under his paws. It was Sully's sweatshirt, the one he usually threw on for early morning walks on the beach with Heathcliff. She sat on the floor beside him and hugged it to her chest. She closed her eyes. A rush of hopelessness filled her. No, nope, nuh-uh. She was not going to give in to it.

A slobbery tongue swooped up the side of her face. She started and opened her eyes. Heathcliff was standing with his nose mere inches from her face. She studied his intelligent brown eyes. "You know something is wrong, don't you?"

He pushed his head against her side. Lindsey reached over and scratched his ears. Zelda let out a plaintive meow, and Lindsey reached up and rubbed her head, too.

"It's going to be all right," she said. "Let's get our phone calls out of the way."

She pulled the chenille throw off the love seat and wrapped it around herself while she took out her phone and called Sully's parents. His mother answered on the second ring.

"Lindsey, is everything all right?" Joan asked. Lindsey suspected that just like her and Heathcliff, Sully's mom had a feeling.

"No," Lindsey said. "I'm so sorry, Joan. But Sully's missing. He was supposed to take the water taxi to bring supplies out to the islands earlier today, as you know, but Ian found his boat drifting in the shallow part of the bay."

There was a murmur in the background, and Lindsey

suspected Sully's dad, Mike, was asking what was happening. She heard Joan repeat what she'd said, and Mike made a low rumble of distress.

"I'm putting you on speakerphone, Lindsey."

"Okay."

"Was he swept overboard?" Joan asked, but then answered her own question. "No, of course not. Sully is too good of a sailor for that sort of thing to happen."

"That's exactly what I thought," Lindsey said. "In fact, I don't think he was ever on his boat."

"What makes you say that?" Mike asked.

"When we went to tie it up, we discovered his boat was cut loose from the dock. They didn't even bother to untie it, and Sully would never do that. Also, his flare gun was intact in his emergency kit. I have a feeling whoever it was who set the boat adrift took Sully."

"Took him?" Joan asked.

Lindsey was aware that she probably sounded daft, but she continued. "I just don't feel like he was on that boat. I can't explain it, but I know he's out there somewhere."

Joan and Mike were silent for a beat. Then Joan said, "I feel the same way."

"Me, too," Mike agreed. "Do you want us to come ashore?"

"In this weather?" Lindsey asked. "No, it's too dangerous. I promise I'll call you first thing when I hear some news. The police chief has already been informed, and she's alerted the Coast Guard. I think the best thing we can do is wait until he comes home. The snow is so thick I didn't even see his truck in the parking lot by the pier, but I'll be checking that as soon as the storm passes and I can get out."

"All right," Mike said. "I'll make some calls to the other islanders just to see if anyone has seen anything suspicious."

"Thank you," Lindsey said. Her voice must have betrayed her worry because her mother-in-law spoke confidently and clearly.

"He's all right, Lindsey," Joan said. "I just know it."

"You're right," Lindsey agreed. "He is and we'll find him. I know we will."

They exchanged good-byes and Lindsey hung up. She could hear the wind howl outside, and when she glanced out, she could see the mounds of snow piling up. She shivered.

A text came in from Emma.

> Coast Guard has been alerted to keep an eye out, and a police patrol boat from a neighboring town is doing a sweep of the shoreline and the islands.

Lindsey texted back a quick thank-you. She should have felt better. Emma was on it. People were looking for Sully. This was all good. But she didn't feel better. She felt terrified. She forwarded the text to her in-laws, hoping that it gave them some peace of mind.

She left the office and headed for the kitchen. Both Heathcliff and Zelda followed her. Not knowing what to do with herself, she picked up the kettle. Where was Sully? Was he out there in the cold? Was he safe? Did he know how to survive in this weather? The worries came as fast as the snow being pelted against the side of the house. She thought about Sully's naval training and knew that if anyone could get through this night, he could. She had to believe in him. She had to believe he would survive.

She stood in the center of the kitchen, holding the kettle, trying not to cry. A feeling of powerlessness overwhelmed her. She wanted to be out there looking for him. If she had to stay here, she was afraid she'd go mad. But given that she always rode her bike to work or Sully dropped her off in his truck, she had no transportation since he'd taken his truck when he left. She wondered how far she could get on foot.

The sound of an engine, a very large low rumbling engine, broke her out of her trance. She put the kettle back down and hurried to the window to see what was happening.

A massive pickup truck was pushing the snow out of her driveway. She wondered if it was one of her neighbors, being helpful. She was about to wave her thanks from the window, when the truck parked and all four doors of the king cab opened. Out stepped the driver, Charlie Peyton, her former downstairs neighbor and a part-time employee of Sully's, and several of the crafternooners—Nancy, Violet and Paula. What were they doing here?

Heathcliff shot out the door to greet some of his favorite people. "Heathcliff! No!"

Lindsey winced as the dog jumped and hugged each person in turn. Thankfully, they all knew to brace themselves for his overabundance of affection. Paula was the first to break away, and she climbed up the porch steps, stomping the snow off her boots as she came.

"Ms. Cole, excuse me, Mayor Cole wanted to come, too, but she's at the town hall dealing with the storm," Paula said. She passed Lindsey in the doorway and entered the house. She kicked off her boots and hung up her jacket. Then she marched into Lindsey's kitchen and put the kettle on as if she knew Lindsey had been about to make a soothing pot of tea.

Lindsey felt a warm burst of hope unfurl inside of her. The sight of her friends calmed her in a way no Earl Grey could.

"Charlene is stuck in New Haven, reporting on the storm," Violet said, hanging up her coat on the rack beside Paula's. "Otherwise she would be here, too."

"Mary called us," Nancy explained. "She and Beth also wanted to be here, but they had to stay with their babies."

"Of course," Lindsey said. She took Nancy's coat and hung it up for her on the coatrack as Nancy had her hands full with a big plastic tub.

"Cowboy cookies," Nancy explained. "Lots of toasted goodness to get you through the rough times."

Lindsey smiled as Nancy joined Paula and Violet in the kitchen. She turned back to Charlie, who stood just inside the door on the doormat, petting Heathcliff. He made no move to take off his coat.

"Need some coffee or tea to warm you up?" she asked.

"No thanks," he said. "I have a thermos full of hot coffee and a bag of cowboy cookies in the truck." He pointed to his snowplow with his thumb. "I'd better get back. I have a lot of roads and driveways to clear."

Charlie Peyton was a thirtysomething musician who rented the apartment above his aunt Nancy. Lindsey had met them both when she rented the apartment above Charlie's in the house that Nancy owned. Nancy had bought the three-story captain's house after she was widowed when her husband, a tugboat captain, went down in a storm.

Lindsey glanced at Nancy in the kitchen. Was the same thing going to happen to her?

"Hey." Charlie nudged her. "Don't think like that. This is Sully. He's going to be fine."

"But—" Lindsey began, but Charlie interrupted her.

"You know what they say about buts," he said. She glanced at him and he added, "Everyone has one."

A tiny smile lifted the corner of her mouth. Leave it to Charlie.

"I have to go, but I'll be back to pick up the ladies," he said. "Do not let Nanners talk you into any wild search and rescue schemes."

"I won't," Lindsey said.

Charlie headed back out into the storm. The wind pulled the door as he stepped out, and he had to use the full weight of his body to close it. A swirl of snow snuck inside and dropped to the foyer floor to melt in tiny little puddles.

Lindsey grabbed a paper towel from the kitchen and cleaned it up so that no one slipped. She then joined her friends in the living room.

"Thank you all for coming," Lindsey said. "But you shouldn't be out in this blizzard."

"Eh." Nancy waved a hand. "I've seen worse." She looked at Violet. "Remember the blizzard of seventy-eight?"

"Do I?" Violet said. "The trees were coated in sheets of ice, the drifts were as high as the houses, it was unforgettable."

Lindsey glanced out the window. "I have a feeling this one will be, too."

Nancy pulled the lid off her tub of cookies and said, "All right, we need some sugar and carbs so we can properly brainstorm. Eat up, ladies."

They each reached for a cookie. Lindsey bit into the decadent oatmeal cookie loaded with toasted coconut, chocolate chips and pecans. Nancy was right. Lindsey could practically feel the synapses in her brain begin to fire.

"All right, what do we know?" Nancy said.

"Sully never got on his boat," Lindsey said. "At least, I don't think he did. Rather, I believe someone grabbed him. They didn't steal his boat. Ian found it floating near shore, which I think means it never made its way out to the islands but was pulled inland by the tide."

"That's so bizarre," Paula said. "Did someone not want him to bring supplies to the islands? Why?"

"I don't think that's it," Lindsey said. "I feel that it must have something to do with the murder of Henry Standish, and the only reason I could think that they'd go after Sully is that he's the perfect distraction. If the murderer can get people looking away from the murder and at the disappearance of a local, then they have time to go into hiding, fix their story or hide any evidence."

"But why Sully?" Violet asked. "They could have grabbed any resident, why him?"

"Because I think they believe he saw something that night on the train. Something he shouldn't have," Lindsey said. She remembered wearing his coat over her pajamas, the ones that matched his, that night and it occurred to her that the person in black whom she'd seen in the passageway might have believed she was Sully the entire time, making Sully the focus of their attention. Oh no.

Violet gasped. "You think he saw the murderer?"

Lindsey shrugged. "No, but it doesn't matter what I think. It's what the murderer thinks. The night that Henry Standish was murdered, I heard noises coming from his compartment. When we went into the passageway to investigate, one of the passengers heard us and came out and yelled at us for making noise. This, of course, brought out a few more of our fellow travelers."

"The passengers who are staying at the inn?" Nancy asked.

Lindsey nodded. "I was about to apologize, when Sully beat me to it. Now that I think about it, anyone in that passageway or anyone in that car could have heard Sully say that he heard some noises and came to investigate, but the truth is that it was me. I was the one who heard the noise and wanted to check it out. Sully just followed me."

She put down her mug and twisted her fingers together. Was that the moment that made Sully a target? She felt ill. She would never be able to live with herself if he'd been harmed because of her.

"Stop that high-speed train right now," Violet said. "You had nothing to do with Sully getting grabbed."

"She's right," Paula agreed. "But since you have a suspect list, let's hear it. Who was in the passageway who might have thought Sully heard something he shouldn't have?"

"Lydia Armand, the one who yelled at us," Lindsey said.

"She took Henry's job as curator of Holden Barclay's private collection."

Violet sat up straight. "I know that name. Barclay dabbled in producing a few Broadway shows, but he was so difficult to work with, people stopped accepting his funding." She tapped her chin with her forefinger. "One of my producers described him as born into wealth, never had a real occupation, consequently, he never developed beyond the willful stage of a toddler with the temperament to match."

Lindsey knew of Holden Barclay because of his extensive collection, but she'd never heard much about the man himself. She tried to picture a woman as assertive as Lydia working for a man known for temper tantrums. It was hard to imagine.

"Who else?" Paula asked. "You said there were several people."

"Penny Minton, Henry's assistant, who he was very cruel to earlier in the dining car. She looked as if she'd just woken up," Lindsey said. She didn't think Penny was that good an actress, but maybe she was. Maybe her performance when Henry had dressed her down in front of everyone was just that, a performance, but to what purpose? She'd have to know it would make her look like a suspect.

"A disgruntled employee is always a person of interest," Nancy said. "Does she strike you as the type who could break her boss's neck?"

The other women all turned to look at Nancy. "What?" She nibbled a cookie. "That's what happened, isn't it?"

"Yes, but how did you know?" Lindsey asked. "I don't think Emma has announced the cause of death publicly."

"I may or may not have friends who work in mass transit," Nancy said.

Lindsey narrowed her eyes. "You know someone who works on the train?"

"My friend Patrick," Nancy said. "He's been a conductor and now a car attendant for years."

"Patrick was our car attendant!" Lindsey cried. "He's the one who went into the compartment and declared Henry deceased."

"I know," Nancy said. "He was very shaken up about it. He called me from the inn, since he knows I live in Briar Creek."

"He has your phone number?" Violet asked.

Paula and Violet exchanged a glance. "It's always the quiet ones you have to watch," Paula said.

"Just how close are you and this Patrick?" Violet asked. She put a hand on her hip. "And why don't I know about him?"

"We're just friends," Nancy said. But there was a wicked twinkle in her eye. "We met when I took the train to Boston for a Red Sox game. He's a fan as well and helped me get off at the right stop."

"He is a very nice man," Lindsey agreed.

"And not a suspect," Nancy added. "He'd certainly have nothing to gain from murdering a passenger."

"Or would he?" Paula asked. Nancy gasped and she said, "I'm just teasing. I'm sure he's an upstanding citizen."

"With a very charming accent," Lindsey added, and was amused to see Nancy's cheeks blossom the faintest shade of pink.

"All right, who else?" Nancy asked. "When we head over to the inn, we'll need to know who to keep an eye on."

"We're going to the inn?" Lindsey asked.

"Yes, of course," Nancy said. "We need to do our civic duty and help the weary travelers, don't you think?"

Lindsey grinned. "You're a scamp."

Nancy returned her smile. "I just find it's sometimes easier to get forgiveness than permission."

"Kirk Duncan," Lindsey said. "He was also in the passageway. It seems he's smitten with Penny and was trying to make up to her for the fact that he wasn't completely honest about who he was when they met."

"Oh, intrigue," Violet said. "I like it. Who else?"

"That was it," Lindsey said. "No, wait, there was also Andrew Shields."

"And what do we know about him?" Paula asked.

"Not much. Sully and I had breakfast with him just before finding Henry," Lindsey said. "The dining car was full and those were the only seats available. Lydia joined us, too."

"If one of them thought Sully knew something and then waited until they could nab him, how would they have gotten around town, especially with the storm coming?" Violet asked.

"Uber?" Paula asked.

They all gave her a look.

"Just spitballing," she said. "But seriously, since none of these people are local and they have to stay at the inn, do you think that's where they're hiding Sully?"

"It makes sense," Violet said.

"Unless they're working with someone on the outside, don't you think?" Nancy asked.

"Or two of them are working together," Violet said.

"We're going to need a reason to go to the inn," Lindsey said.

"I'd say you have plenty of reason," Paula said. "Looking for your husband being number one, but bringing books to entertain our poor snowbound guests being another."

"Oh, that's a brilliant cover," Lindsey said. "And really perfect since they're all book people. Do you really think whoever took Sully is hiding him at the inn?"

"If it has to do with the murder on the train, that makes the most sense," Nancy nodded. "All of the known suspects are at the inn, and whoever it is would want to keep a close eye on him."

Lindsey glanced out at the howling wind. "You're right. I don't want to wait until morning. If Sully is at the inn, I want to look for him tonight."

Her friends watched her. Then Nancy nodded. "As soon as Charlie gets back, he can drive us all there in the truck."

Lindsey felt the bands of anxiety that had been coiled about her chest ease. She knew Emma was going to be unhappy, but if she had to choose between an angry police chief and sitting here all night fretting, she'd take the police chief hands down.

\*   \*   \*

I don't think this is a good idea," Charlie said. He was in the driver's seat with Lindsey riding shotgun while Violet, Nancy and Paula shared the back seat.

The snow was still coming down. Visibility was terrible, but the truck was cranking out the heat, for which Lindsey was grateful. Heathcliff and Zelda had been clearly confused to see her go back out into the blizzard, but she promised she'd be home as soon as she could with Sully. Heathcliff's eyebrows moved up and down, which she took as approval for her mission.

"Well, I can't sit home and do nothing," Lindsey said.

"Yes, but the chief . . ." Charlie glanced at her with wide eyes.

"I can handle Emma," Lindsey said. It was a big fat fib, but mercifully no one called her on it. She had Charlie stop at the library. She and Paula quickly ducked in through the back door and grabbed books off the shelves that they thought their "guests" might like. They came out to discover that Charlie had plowed the library parking lot while they were gone.

"Excellent." Paula clapped him on the shoulder. "If we actually open tomorrow, this will make it much easier to access the building."

"Maybe," Charlie said. He glanced out the window at the village blanketed by well over a foot of snow. "I don't know about you all, but I feel as if the snow is never going to stop. Ever."

He heaved a sigh and set a course for the inn. Once they had left the main road, he dropped his plow, removing the thick coating of snow from the winding road that led to Michelle's place. The parking lot was empty except for Robbie's car and Emma's police cruiser.

"Okay, here's what I think we should do," Nancy said. "Charlie, you keep plowing the lot. We'll go inside and say that you were taking us home but had to make a side trip to plow out the parking area. We thought we'd come in and get warm and 'oh, hey, look at the books we just happen to have.'"

"That's your plan?" Violet asked.

"You have a better one?" Nancy asked.

"Yes," Violet said. "I find in cases of emergency, one can always get sympathy if the need for a restroom has become dire."

Nancy blinked at her. "Oh, you are good. That's even better. No one would question why two ladies of a certain age need to use the facilities. Let's go."

With that, Nancy hopped out of the truck cab and held the door open for the others. Lindsey turned in her seat and said, "Thanks, Charlie. I'll call you if we need a ride immediately, but feel free to go ahead with your plowing."

"I'll keep my phone handy," he said. "It goes without saying, if you find Sully—"

"I'll call you right away," she said. She turned to step out of the truck.

"Hey, Lindsey," Charlie called after her. "Be careful."

"Promise," she said. She slammed the door behind her,

hauling the big bag of books she carried over her shoulder like Santa with a sack full of toys. She followed her friends to the front door of the inn.

Paula knocked, and in moments, Michelle unlocked and opened the door. She stared at them. "What . . . how?"

"Charlie was bringing us home," Nancy said. "But I needed to make a pit stop."

"Me, too," Violet added. "The cold, you know."

"Of course, come in." Michelle ushered them all inside. "Do you know where it is?"

"Just around the corner," Nancy said.

"That's right." Michelle nodded.

"I remember from election night when Ms. Cole was voted in as mayor," Nancy said. "That was a fun party."

"It sure was," Paula said.

Nancy disappeared around the corner and they settled in to wait.

There was a log fire burning in the fireplace in the lobby, and Lindsey moved over to stand beside it while Violet waited for her turn to use the facilities.

"Is there anything else I can get you?" Michelle asked.

"No, thank you," Lindsey said. "Charlie had to go and plow a nearby street, but he said he'd be back to pick us up shortly."

Michelle studied her, and Lindsey got the feeling the other woman knew there was more going on than she was saying, but she just smiled and went back to her seat behind the check-in desk.

A door on the far end of the lobby opened, and Chief

Plewicki strode into the lobby. She took one look at Lindsey and asked, "Did something happen? Did you hear from Sully?"

"No." Lindsey's voice sounded wobbly and she cleared her throat. She needed to appear assertive if she was going to stand her ground with Emma.

"What are you doing here?"

"We were getting a ride with Charlie, but Nancy needed to use a facility," Violet said. "Me, too, for that matter. The cold, you know."

Emma's eyes narrowed and she asked, "And what's in the bags?"

"Books," Lindsey said enthusiastically as if they were the answer to all of life's problems, which to her they were.

CHAPTER

13

BRIAR CREEK
PUBLIC LIBRARY

Emma planted one hand on her hip and waved Lindsey over to her side. In a low voice so that the others couldn't hear, she said, "Want to tell me what's really going on?"

"Yes, actually, I was hoping you'd have a second to talk," Lindsey said.

Violet and Paula pretended not to be listening, but even Violet's Tony Award–winning acting talents couldn't cover the way she had an ear cocked in their direction.

"I'm listening," Emma said.

"I think someone on the train thinks Sully saw or heard something they didn't want him to, and I think they grabbed him because they're afraid he might know something," she said. "And because all of the passengers in question are here, I think Sully is here somewhere, too."

Emma leaned back and stared at her with wide eyes. "Are you serious?"

Before Lindsey could answer, the lights went out.

Michelle let out a mild curse and said, "I'll bet it's a circuit breaker. I need to go down to the basement and check it out."

"Let me make sure the building is secure first," Emma said.

Michelle bent down behind the desk and came up with a flashlight and a toolbox. "Standing by," she agreed.

There was a shriek from somewhere in the building, and Lindsey felt the hair on the back of her neck rise.

"Nobody leave this room!" Emma ordered. She grabbed her radio and began speaking into it as she strode in the direction of the staircase that would bring her upstairs. "Kirkland, what's your twenty?"

His voice crackled in return, and it sounded as if he said he was up on the second floor.

The flames in the fireplace cast the room in an amber glow that would have been lovely any other time, but at the moment, the flickering light of the fire sent deep, dark shadows dancing against the walls, and it was, frankly, terrifying.

Lindsey's phone chimed. It was Charlie. She put it on speaker. "What's happening in there?"

"The power went out," Lindsey said. "Can you see if there is power in any buildings nearby?"

She felt Violet and Paula press closer to her, and she could tell they were nervous, too.

"The houses nearby still have their lights on, it's just the inn," he said. "Do you want me to come in?"

"No," Lindsey said. "Michelle's going to check the circuit breaker, and Emma and Officer Kirkland are here. We're okay."

"Where's Nanners?" Charlie asked. His voice was tight with concern.

"I'm right here," Nancy said as she reentered the room. "Nice and toasty by the fire, don't you worry."

"Okay," Charlie said. "I'll stay in the area. Call me if you need me."

"Will do," Lindsey said. She glanced over at the check-in desk and said, "Charlie says it's just the inn that's without power."

Michelle frowned. "That's odd. I'm going down to check the panel."

"Do you want me to go with you?"

"It's down in the basement," Michelle said.

"That's okay," Lindsey said. "I don't mind."

"If you're sure," Michelle said. "I know Emma said to wait, but if I can have the power back on in minutes, why not try?"

Lindsey glanced at the others. "Tell Emma we're in the basement."

She tried to hide her enthusiasm. This was just the opportunity she needed. If Sully was being kept somewhere in the inn, the basement would be a perfect location. Nancy, Violet and Paula gave her knowing thumbs-ups, and Lindsey knew they were hoping the exact same thing.

"We'll hold the fort," Nancy said.

"Don't you worry," Violet replied.

"We've got this," Paula added.

Lindsey sent them a wide-eyed look, hoping they weren't overselling their willingness to sit in the near dark so that she could go and snoop. Michelle was checking her toolbox and didn't notice.

"All right, I think I have everything I could possibly need, let's go." Michelle handed Lindsey one of two flash-lights and said, "Follow me."

They left the lobby, striding down the main hall of the inn, toward the kitchen. Michelle explained, "The base-ment door is in the kitchen."

"Of course," Lindsey said. She followed, leaving some space between them so she could shine her light into each room as they passed. She couldn't do more than a cursory sweep, but she found it hard to believe that Sully would be in one of the rooms on the first floor. He'd be found entirely too easily.

Her flashlight beam darted across the kitchen. Pots and pans hung from a circular rack hanging over the stove, and the apparatus cast a huge shadow on the ceiling that loomed over them like a monster. Lindsey found it very unsettling.

The kitchen smelled of industrial cleaner with faint traces of rosemary and garlic and something fried. Lindsey wondered if the smells had anything to do with the wed-ding that should have taken place earlier in the day. Had the couple with the canceled wedding left behind their wedding cake? Because stress eating some cake right now felt like a great idea. She shook her head, trying to regain her focus.

Michelle stopped at a door in the back of the kitchen. She pulled it open and it creaked on its old hinges, which seemed very loud in the silence.

"I suppose that's one more thing to add to my to-do list," Michelle said. "Oil hinges."

"Owning a place this large must be like maintaining a never-ending list," Lindsey said.

"It is endless," Michelle said. "Thankfully, I have a terrific handyman who comes whenever I need him, even in the middle of the night. Of course, I would never call him out in a storm like this even if he is better with the electricity than I am."

Michelle led the way, and they started down the open wood staircase, holding the handrail as they went. The air was musty and frigid, and it was so dark that even their flashlights had a hard time illuminating the gloom. The floor of the basement was concrete, and Lindsey was relieved to step on it. She shone her light around and noted the basement seemed to be mostly storage with old dressers, bedframes, dishes and assorted other household goods.

"Please excuse the mess," Michelle said. "I keep promising myself I'm going to clean it out, but I simply haven't had time. Plus, I'm always afraid that the minute I throw something out, I'll need it the next day."

Lindsey smiled. She knew the feeling. They shuffled

carefully around the piles of stuff toward the far wall. Michelle shone her light right on the big gray metal box mounted on the wall. Lindsey recognized it as a circuit breaker panel. That was about as far as her knowledge extended and she hoped that the panel didn't require someone with expert skill.

Michelle flipped open the lid. She ran her beam of light up and down over the breakers. "I'll be damned. Those breakers were manually switched off."

"How do you know?" Lindsey asked.

"Because in a power outage, the breakers stay on even though the power is out," Michelle said. "But every breaker for the entire inn is in the off position. That had to be done manually."

"You don't have any recently fired employees with a grudge, do you?" Lindsey asked.

"No," Michelle said. "I keep a very small staff who are like family. Why?"

"Just wondering," Lindsey said. If the staff of the inn were out of the equation, then it only stood to reason that whoever did this was tied to the murder investigation.

Michelle started snapping the switches back on. Once she'd flipped them all, they headed back through the basement until they reached the stairs. Michelle tapped the light switch on, and the basement was flooded with light from the overhead fluorescents.

"Let there be light," she said. She switched it back off, and they trudged up the stairs to the main floor, which was now bathed in light. Michelle took a long breath and said,

"That's a relief. I didn't want to have to call an electrician in the middle of a blizzard."

They walked through the kitchen back to the lobby. Emma was waiting there, and she looked unhappy.

"What do you think you're doing?" Emma asked.

"We were down in the basement, turning the power back on," Michelle said. She seemed unperturbed by Emma's tone, whereas Lindsey was looking anywhere but at Emma. She'd been in the hot seat with the chief of police enough to know how unpleasant it was.

"And what if there was a murderer down in the basement?" Emma asked.

"He now has enough light to see what he's doing," Michelle said. Her tone was wry but Emma was not amused.

"Cookie?" Nancy asked. She'd brought her tub of cowboy cookies with them and shoved the plastic container in between Emma and Michelle.

Michelle smiled and reached in. Emma huffed a disgruntled noise and did the same. Nancy beamed at Violet, who sent her a thumbs-up.

"What was the yell we heard after the lights went out?" Lindsey asked.

"Lydia Armand thought she saw a person dressed in a black coat in her room," Emma said. "We searched all the rooms on her floor, but there was no sign of anyone. Kirkland is checking the floor above. Despite going against my explicit instructions, your timing with the lights is appreciated."

Michelle nodded as if she knew how much Emma loathed admitting it. "No problem."

"A person in a black coat?" Lindsey asked.

"Yes, why? Did you see someone like that?"

"Not here, not tonight," Lindsey said. "But remember the person I saw in the passageway on the train the night that Henry Standish was murdered was also in a black coat."

Emma bit into her cookie and chewed while she considered Lindsey. "Can you remember anything else about them?"

"I didn't see any distinctive features. I couldn't tell you if it was a man or a woman, how old they were, really nothing significant because in addition to the black coat, they wore a black hat and scarf."

"How tall?" Emma asked.

"About six feet, give or take, but I don't know if they were wearing heels of any kind. It was too hard to see."

"Build?"

"Medium?" Lindsey answered it like a question, and Emma stared at her. "Medium to slender."

"That matches what Lydia described," Emma said.

Violet gasped. "That means the killer is here at the inn."

"Whoa, whoa, whoa, I did not sign on for that when I agreed to feed and house the train passengers," Michelle said. She crossed her arms over her chest.

"Let's not jump to conclusions," Emma said. "First, we don't know if the person Lindsey saw is the murderer."

"But it seems likely," Nancy said.

Emma shrugged. "A long black coat in New England is not that unusual. Besides, whoever it was disappeared before we got upstairs. We only have Lydia's word for it that she even saw what she said she saw."

"Oh, right, because if she was the one in the black coat on the train, it would behoove her to say she saw someone like that in the inn and take the heat off herself," Paula said.

Emma shrugged. "Or she actually did see someone in her room dressed all in black."

"And the lights conveniently went out, allowing the person to escape," Lindsey said. She knew she sounded skeptical, but truly, what were the odds that Lydia would see the same person Lindsey saw and then the power would go out?

"Given that the circuit breakers were manually switched off one by one, that seems unlikely," Michelle said.

"Were they? Huh. It's only unlikely if we assume Henry's murderer is working alone," Emma said. "It seems to me, with so much money at stake over a rare first edition, that whoever murdered Henry is potentially working for someone who is willing to pay any price to have that book."

"But then why risk losing the book by planting it on me?" Lindsey asked.

"When they realized Henry would be discovered and the train stopped, they must have panicked and tried to ditch the evidence, and you were a convenient receptacle. They probably thought they'd get it back before you found it, but maybe the blizzard changed their plans," Emma said. She gave Lindsey a hard stare. "Any sign of Sully in the basement?"

"No." Lindsey shook her head.

"I've got Kirkland and Robbie checking every room upstairs for him," Emma said. "If he's here, we'll find him, and we'll call you."

It was clear they were being dismissed.

"We brought some books for the passengers," Paula said. As a stalling tactic, it was so-so.

"Much appreciated," Emma said. She held her arms wide and said, "Now it's time to get on home before the blizzard makes it impossible for you to leave. Call Charlie and tell him to pick you up."

"But—" Lindsey felt as if Emma was blocking her one chance to find Sully. He had to be here somewhere. He just had to.

"Don't make me lock you up for impeding an investigation," Emma said.

"You wouldn't," Lindsey said.

"Wouldn't I?" Emma asked.

They stared at each other, and Lindsey knew she couldn't risk it. She nodded once. Emma would absolutely lock her up, and they both knew it.

Nancy took her cell phone out of her pocket and fired off a text to Charlie. In minutes, he was parked in front of the inn, waiting to pick them up.

They suited up for the weather and started for the door. Emma held Lindsey back with a hand on her arm.

"Be careful," she cautioned her. "Whoever took Sully is probably the same person who hid the book inside your bag. You two are on the killer's radar, and we have no idea what they're planning next."

CHAPTER

14

BRIAR CREEK
PUBLIC LIBRARY

G ot it," Lindsey said. Emma gave her arm a quick squeeze
and let her go.

Lindsey stepped back out into the biting cold and
shivered. She hated leaving the inn when it felt as if it was
the only connection she had to finding her husband. Where
was Sully? Who had taken him and why? She had to believe
it had something to do with the train. If only she had cor-
rected him on the train and said she was the one who'd heard
the noises coming from Henry's compartment. If only.

They were silent on the ride home in the snowplow.
Charlie dropped them off one by one, leaving Lindsey for
last since he had to plow the side roads in her neighborhood
again. As he pulled into her driveway, his headlights illuminated the front of her house.

"Lindsey, is that Heathcliff?" he asked. He pointed at

the front door, and a hairy black fur ball, covered in snow, barked.

"Heathcliff!" Lindsey shoved open her door and hopped out of the truck. She ran across the front yard, her feet slipping in the snow. Heathcliff didn't leave the small porch, which was the first indication that something was dreadfully wrong. Heathcliff always ran at his people with one hundred percent enthusiasm. Just like before when she'd found him with Sully's shirt, she knew her boy was upset.

Lindsey dropped to her knees beside him. His fur was covered in snow, and he was shivering. She wrapped her arms around him, and Heathcliff licked her cheek. Even his tongue was cold. She turned around to find Charlie right behind her. "He's freezing. Help me get him inside."

She yanked off her glove and reached into her pocket for her house key. Charlie reached past her, turned the knob and pushed the door open. It hadn't been locked! Heat poured out at them, and Heathcliff gingerly stepped inside and shook the snow off his fur. It scatted across the foyer and he dropped to the floor and began to lick and bite his feet.

"I'm going to grab some towels and blankets," Lindsey said. "See if you can get him to move to the living room by the radiator."

She scanned the living room, looking at the spot on the convector where Zelda liked to bake her bones. She was stretched out full length, soaking up the heat. Lindsey exhaled in relief. At least she hadn't gotten out, too.

Lindsey hurried down the hallway to the linen closet.

She grabbed a towel and blanket and dashed back to the living room. Charlie had dragged Heathcliff's dog bed in front of the heater where Zelda slept, and Heathcliff had climbed into it. She tossed Charlie a towel.

"If you'll dry his fur, I'll warm up his feet," she said. They set to work, with Lindsey talking to Heathcliff the entire time. "My poor boy. What happened? How did you get outside?"

Heathcliff nudged her hands with his cold nose. She got the feeling he'd tell her everything if he could. When she had his feet warmed up and he stopped shivering, Lindsey went to get him some food and water. Charlie stayed with him, keeping an arm around Heathcliff to keep him warm.

When Lindsey put down his food, Heathcliff ate, pausing to drink before eating more. It was then that she knew he was going to be fine. She sat back on her heels.

"He's going to be okay," she said.

"Yeah, our boy's a champ," Charlie agreed. He patted Heathcliff's back.

"How could I have been so irresponsible to not have locked the door?" she asked. "I was certain I locked it before we left, but how did he get out?" She glanced at her dog. "Have you learned how to open doors? Because if you have, that's a problem."

"You did lock it," Charlie said. "I saw you."

"Did I not close the door all the way?"

Charlie shook his head. "No, I watched you lock the door from the truck and you jiggled the handle. You would have noticed."

"Would I?" Lindsey asked. "I was so distracted."

"Lindsey, I think someone broke into your house," Charlie said. "Well, if they didn't break and enter, they definitely just entered."

"But where?" She glanced at the sliding glass doors that looked over the backyard and the beach beyond. Could she and Sully have left it unlocked when they arrived home? It was highly probable.

She hopped up from the floor and checked the sliding glass doors. Sure enough, it was unlocked. She flicked on the outside light to see if there were any tracks in the snow. It was still falling heavily and the wind was so strong that if there had been any impressions, they'd been swept away into drifts along the side of the house.

She turned around and scanned the room. If someone had broken into the house, there was only one reason that they'd done it, and that was to retrieve the book that they'd shoved into Lindsey's bag. She hurried down the hall to her bedroom, where she found that their bags had been thoroughly ransacked.

Their carry-on roller bags were unzipped and the contents strewn all over the floor. She looked for her laptop bag and discovered it open with the items inside half hanging out, including her laptop.

She didn't touch anything but hurried back to the living room, where she grabbed her cell phone and called Emma.

The police chief answered on the third ring. "What?"

"Emma, someone broke into my house, well, maybe not broke in, but they definitely entered, and the bags Sully and

I took on our trip were ransacked. Also, they let Heathcliff out of the house, and Charlie and I found him on the front steps, shivering in the cold."

Lindsey's voice cracked on the last part and Emma cried, "They left Heathcliff out in this blizzard? Is he all right?"

Lindsey glanced over at her dog, who was swaddled in a thick fluffy blanket and nestled down in his bed. As she watched, Zelda hopped off the radiator cover and climbed into the dog bed with her buddy. The two of them snuggled up under the blanket together. Charlie looked at her with an *aw* expression.

"Yeah, he's okay," she said. She would have wallowed in the glorious feeling of relief if it weren't for the fact that her husband was still missing.

"Don't touch anything," Emma ordered. "In fact, is Charlie still there?"

"Yes."

"Good. Pack up Heathcliff and Zelda and a bag for yourself and have Charlie bring you back to the inn," Emma ordered.

"But—" Lindsey started to protest.

"No." Emma shut her right down. "You're not safe there. The pets aren't safe there. And I want the crime lab to come in with a fingerprint kit and crawl all over your house. Touch as little as possible and get here pronto."

"Okay—" Lindsey began, but Emma had already hung up. Lindsey lowered the phone and said, "Would you mind driving me and the kids back to the inn?"

"Not at all." Charlie glanced out the window. "The roads that need plowing aren't going anywhere."

Lindsey followed the line of his gaze. The wind was howling, the snow blowing and the temperature dropping. He was right. She nodded and went to pack.

Within minutes, Lindsey and Charlie were back in the snowplow with Heathcliff buckled in the back seat and Zelda in her carrier. Neither of them were happy to be out in the cold, but Lindsey thought going back to the inn with Heathcliff was genius. If anyone could find Sully, it was Heathcliff.

The drive was slow. The roads were turning into sheets of ice, and Charlie tried to pick his route by determining which roads had been plowed and sanded. They had to take the long way around.

When they arrived, Michelle was still seated at the front desk. She glanced up when the door opened and Lindsey strode in with Heathcliff at her side and Zelda in a cat carrier.

"Emma told me what happened," she said. She came around the desk and dropped to the ground. She held out her hand to Heathcliff, who nudged it with his nose. "Are you okay, buddy?"

Heathcliff wagged and leaned into her, accepting her back scratches with enthusiasm.

"He seems okay," Lindsey said. She glanced at Charlie, who carried in her duffel bag with her overnight things. "Thanks."

"No problem," he said. "Call me if you need anything or if there's any word on Sully."

"I will," she said.

He paused to pat Heathcliff's head before stepping back out into the storm.

"Come on, I'll show you to your room, and you can get the critters settled," Michelle said. She picked up the bag Charlie had put on the floor. "I only have two rooms left and they're both on the first floor."

"Great," Lindsey said. She shed her hat and scarf as they walked down the hallway. Her room was halfway down and on the left. Michelle used a key card to unlock it. She opened the door and stepped aside for Lindsey to enter with the cat carrier after Heathcliff, who bounded inside with a dog's enthusiasm of being in a new place with new smells.

The room was done in soft shades of blue and gray, with gray carpet and pale blue walls and a bedspread that pulled both shades together. The sliding glass doors on the far side of the room looked out over the pool, which was covered for the winter, and the boardwalk that led through the dunes to the beach beyond. Neither the dunes nor the beach was visible through the darkness, but Lindsey knew they were there just the same. She checked the lock on the door, feeling a heightened sense of security.

"Will this do?" Michelle asked.

"More than," Lindsey said. "Thanks for letting me bring the pets. I appreciate it."

"No problem, I get it," Michelle said. "I had dogs and cats while growing up. They're family."

Lindsey glanced at Heathcliff and Zelda. Yes, they were.

"I'll be in the lobby if you need anything," she said.

"I'll be out as soon as they're settled," Lindsey said. "I need to talk to Emma."

"Last I heard, she was interviewing persons of interest again," Michelle said. "I think she's hoping to get a lead on Sully's whereabouts. I'm so sorry. I know you must be worried."

If she didn't talk about it, she was okay, but the second someone expressed sympathy, Lindsey felt the panic she'd been keeping a lid on bubble up in her chest. Sully. Where was he? She knew her husband well enough to know that if he was able to get home, he would have by now.

She nodded, and Michelle gave her a small smile of encouragement as she left, closing the door behind her.

Lindsey knelt down beside the cat carrier. Zelda turned her back to her, and Lindsey couldn't blame her. She had been pushed out of her cozy nest with Heathcliff and put in a carrier and taken out into the howling wind and cold. But Lindsey couldn't leave her in the house alone with a bunch of crime scene techs or, worse, the same person who broke in before showing up again.

She reached in and took Zelda out. She sat on the floor and held her in her lap. She stroked her fur exactly where Zelda liked it, and the tension slowly eased out of the cat until she stepped out of Lindsey's lap into a full-body stretch. Heathcliff was busy sniffing every inch of the room, getting a bead on every person and pet who had stayed there before them.

Lindsey glanced at the time on her phone. She waited impatiently while they acclimated. When Zelda hopped up onto the armchair where Lindsey had thrown her puffy coat and began to knead, she knew the cat was going to be okay if she left her alone for a bit.

Heathcliff, on the other hand, sat beside her with his black ears cocked and his tongue hanging out between his lips. She suspected he was not going to be so easily left behind. But if her theory was right, and Sully was somewhere in the inn, then Heathcliff would be the one to find him. She reached over and patted his head.

"Are you up for it, buddy?"

Heathcliff licked her wrist. She glanced at Zelda, who was burrowed into Lindsey's coat. A soft snore sounded, and Lindsey took that as permission to leave.

She checked the window and the sliding glass doors. Both were locked. She left one of the bedside lamps on and took her phone and her key card with her. She glanced down at Heathcliff.

"Let's go find him," she said.

They left the room, and she paused to check and make certain the door locked behind them. Lindsey strode down the hallway to the check-in desk. The fire was still crackling despite the late hour, and Michelle sat at her desk, looking exhausted. It had been a full day. She had to be bone weary.

"Where's Emma?" she asked.

Michelle pointed to the stairs beyond the desk. "Second floor. Room 201."

"Any chance you'll be able to get some sleep?" Lindsey asked.

"I sent all of my staff home," Michelle said. "No one needs to be out in this storm, and with the police on the premises, I figured I can handle it by myself. I'll catch a cat nap when everyone settles for the night."

"You've met Emma, right?" Lindsey teased.

"Even Emma has to sleep at some point," Michelle said.

Lindsey watched as Heathcliff scouted out the lobby. If Sully had been in here, he didn't smell him.

"Well, I know absolutely nothing about being a night manager at an inn," Lindsey said. "But I'm willing to take a shift on the desk so you can get some rest."

"Thanks," Michelle said. "I appreciate the offer, and I'm tired enough that I'll keep it in mind."

Lindsey turned and headed for the staircase, with Heathcliff falling into step beside her. The steps wound up to the second floor, where there was a small sitting area with a coffee table, a love seat and several plush chairs all upholstered in the same blue gray as her room.

Two hallways led out of the landing, and Lindsey checked the room numbers. She turned left, following the numbers to room 201. It was the first room on the left, and she could hear the sound of voices as she approached. She wondered if she should wait outside, but Emma had told her to check in when she arrived, so she lifted her fist and knocked.

The voices went quiet and the door opened. Emma took her in at a glance. "I'm glad you're here. Come in."

Lindsey entered and saw that Andrew Shields was sitting on the love seat. Officer Wilcox was in the room, leaning against the far wall. Lindsey assumed Officer Kirkland was out monitoring the rest of the guests in the inn.

The wind howled against the window, and Lindsey shivered even though there was no draft. Again, her mind flitted to Sully. Where was he? Who had cut his boat free? And why? She shook her head, refusing to let her worry take over. Sully would be found. He would be okay.

"Lindsey, don't tell me the investigation has forced you to stay here as well," Andrew said. "It must be very frustrating when you live in town and could be home."

Lindsey glanced at Emma. She knew the chief well enough to know she wouldn't want her to discuss the fact that her house had been broken into or that her husband was missing.

"Something like that," she said. She reached down and patted Heathcliff's head. Having him beside her grounded her.

"Sorry to hear it," he said. He turned to Emma. "I'm assuming you want to question her and I'm free to go?" There was a barely concealed annoyance in his voice.

Emma tipped her chin up and said, "Of course, just remind me again of where it is you work."

"The Library of Congress," he said. "I'm sure you've heard of it."

"And your boss's name?" Emma pressed, ignoring his sarcasm.

"Gladys Metzger," he said.

"And what is it that you do there?" Emma asked.

"I appraise and acquire materials for a special collection at the direction of my supervisor," he said.

"Ms. Metzger?" Emma asked.

"Yes." Andrew sighed. "Am I having déjà vu, or have we had this exact same conversation three times?"

"Just making certain I've got it straight." Emma smiled at him. "So many archivists, so many libraries. Lots to keep track of, but I'm sure you understand."

Andrew's eyes narrowed as if he couldn't decide if she was mocking him or not.

"Thank you for your time," Emma said. "Officer Wilcox, please escort Mr. Shields back to his room."

Wilcox pushed off the wall and strode across the room, falling into step beside Andrew.

Andrew paused beside Lindsey and muttered, "You might want to ask for a cup of coffee. Trust me, this will be one of the most boring conversations you've ever had."

"Perhaps," she said. "Out of curiosity from one archivist to another, which collection at the Library of Congress do you work on?"

Andrew's eyebrows lifted. "What do you mean?"

"Well, there's so many collections, which one is yours?" Lindsey stared at him. She was getting a very weird feeling off Andrew. She felt Heathcliff move from sitting to standing, pressing against her side, as if he, too, sensed something was off.

Andrew sent her a grin and said, "Well, the rare books collection, obviously."

"Oh, of course." Lindsey returned his grin. "Gladys Metzger must be in charge of the Hewitt Collection, then. Silly me, how could I have forgotten? You must love working there, such an incredible special collection."

"It is," Andrew agreed. The tension in his shoulders eased. "I feel very fortunate."

"Which is weird." She turned to Emma and said, "Because there is no Hewitt Collection in the Library of Congress, I made it up."

CHAPTER

15

BRIAR CREEK
PUBLIC LIBRARY

S ay that again," Emma said. She held up her hand at Officer Wilcox and said, "Wait."

Lindsey took her phone out and opened up a search engine. She typed in the collections and turned the screen so
that Emma could see. "No Hewitt Collection."

"How do you know these things?" Emma asked.

"Librarian," Lindsey said. "Plus, I did an internship with
the Library of Congress and got very familiar with all of
their collections."

"So, Mr. Shields, if you aren't an archivist at the Library
of Congress, who are you?" Emma asked.

"You actually believe her over me?" he asked. "A small-
town librarian who hasn't worked in the industry in years?"

Emma glanced between them. "Yup." She jerked her

head in the direction of the room. "Back inside. Let's take this interview from the top."

"You're wasting your time," he said. "I have nothing to do with any of this, and I refuse to talk."

"Then you'll find yourself moved from the comfort of the inn to your own cell at the jail," Emma said.

"I've stayed in worse places," he countered.

Sensing the hostility in the exchange, Heathcliff began to growl. Lindsey stroked his head, trying to soothe him.

"If you want, I can wait outside," she said to Emma.

"That might be best. I'll walk you out," Emma offered. She led the way out of the room and into the hallway, where she closed the door behind them.

"What did you want to see me about?" Lindsey asked.

"Sadly nothing as helpful as the information you just handed us," she said. "I just wanted to apprise you that the crime scene techs are at your house, and while they might be done in an hour give or take, I still think you should spend the night here at the inn because of the blizzard."

Lindsey glanced down at Heathcliff, who was sniffing the air as if getting a bead on the place. She didn't want to drag him and Zelda back out in the dead of night. And she wanted to stay as close to the police as possible while the investigation into Sully's disappearance was ongoing. She wanted to ask for an update but she also didn't want to know, so she just waited.

"The police boat searching the islands hasn't found anything," Emma said. "Neither has the Coast Guard."

Lindsey sagged at the knees. "That's good news."

"I'm choosing to take it that way."

"Then I will, too," Lindsey said.

"Go get some sleep," Emma said. "If there's any news, I'll tell you right away."

"Same," Lindsey said.

"No, no, no," Emma said. "There will be no news from you because you are going to your room and you are going right to sleep, correct?"

"Correct," Lindsey said. She put just enough reluctance in her voice to make it clear that she wasn't going willingly.

"Good." Emma gave her a quick nod and turned back to the door. She paused, resting her hand on the doorknob. "If you had to guess what our friend Andrew's real occupation is, what would you say?"

"I don't know. That's tricky," Lindsey said. "I mean, why would he say he was an archivist? I guess we have to consider what sort of occupations require a cover?"

"Good observation," Emma said. Over her shoulder she added, "To your room."

"Got it," Lindsey said. She waited until the door shut before she headed in the opposite direction of the stairs. Oh, she was going to her room, but she fully intended to take the scenic route.

She led Heathcliff down the hallway. "All right, buddy, do you smell Sully?"

The dog didn't answer but his ears pricked up, and he continued to sniff the air as if he were looking for evidence that Sully was there. Lindsey tried not to get too hopeful. Heathcliff wasn't a tracker, after all. But if anyone could find Sully in this building, she was confident he would.

They strode all the way to the end, where the fire escape stairs were located beyond a steel door. She hesitated, not knowing if it was alarmed. She decided it was worth the risk and popped the latch. If she were a kidnapper, hiding her hostage in a stairwell seemed like a solid idea to her.

She pushed the door open as quietly as she could. She made a *shh* noise to Heathcliff, and he padded into the stairwell almost soundlessly. It wouldn't have mattered anyway because there were people in the stairwell talking so loudly that they couldn't hear them.

Lindsey grabbed Heathcliff's collar, while at the same time she wedged her foot in the door to keep it from slamming shut. She slowly lowered herself into a crouch as she strained to hear.

"I have nothing to say to you, Kirk," a female voice said. "You have made a mess of everything."

"Everything I've done has been for you," a male voice protested, presumably Kirk Duncan's, unless there was another man named Kirk down there.

"Ha, that's rich," the woman scoffed. It sounded like a lovers' quarrel, which indicated it was Penny. Lindsey remembered how the two of them had chatted so flirtatiously at dinner on the train. Maybe Kirk had finally gotten Penny to talk to him. "You're obsessed with that book. That's all you care about."

"That's not true," he protested. "I care about you, I do."

"Then you need to prove it," Penny sobbed. Her voice became muffled, and Lindsey imagined she was in his arms crying against his shirtfront.

"I will," he said. "I'd do anything for you."

Clearly, Penny was finally going to give Kirk another chance. Lindsey didn't know whether to be pleased for the young woman or worried. What if Kirk was Henry's killer? What if he really was only interested in the book? Then again, should she be worried for Kirk? What if Penny was the killer because Henry had been such a demanding boss? It was too much. Her head hurt.

"I love you," he said.

"I love you, too," she replied.

There was the distinct sound of passionate kissing.

Now that the moment had become horrifically awkward, Lindsey decided to do a full retreat. She rose from her crouched position and opened the door so that she could slip through. She backed into the hallway, pulling Heathcliff with her, and closed the door gently behind her. She let go of his collar and straightened up when a voice behind her said, "Something interesting in the stairwell?"

"Yah!" Lindsey yelped and whipped around. "Robbie!" she cried, and put a hand over her heart. "You scared the life out of me."

"Really?" he asked. He reached down to pet Heathcliff, who was bouncing on his feet at the sight of one of his favorite people. "You look all right, a bit peaky, but still kicking."

A small smile passed over Lindsey's lips. "I feel worse than a bit peaky."

"I know," he said. "I just talked to Emma, and she told me that the Coast Guard and police patrol boat haven't spotted anything."

"Not that they could in this storm," Lindsey said. "But I still don't believe he was ever on that boat."

"It doesn't seem likely," Robbie agreed. "Are you and Heathcliff sniffing out the inn?"

Lindsey glanced away. "Maybe."

The door to the stairwell opened, and Kirk stepped through. He looked startled at the sight of Lindsey and Robbie, as if he'd expected the hallway to be empty. Lindsey noted two spots of color high on his cheeks. She couldn't determine whether it was embarrassment or something else, something she didn't want to dwell on.

He was wearing a heavy coat and boots, and his hat and gloves were clutched in his hands. She'd thought he'd just met up with Penny in the stairwell, but his clothing indicated he'd been outside. In this weather? Where? And why?

As if correctly interpreting her thoughts, he said, "Just popped out for a smoke. Not worth it. Brr." He shivered. She noticed there was no scent of tobacco smoke coming off him, but maybe he hadn't lingered.

"Oh," she said. "I'm just taking my dog for a walk." She stepped to the side, pulling Robbie and Heathcliff with her.

"Be careful. It's brutal out there," Kirk said. He nodded at them and continued down the hallway. He paused in front of a door and used his key card to open it. He went inside, letting the door slam shut behind him.

"He seems intense," Robbie said.

"He was just making out with Penny," Lindsey said. "Or as you call it 'snogging.'"

"And how do we know this?" Robbie asked.

"I was stepping into the stairwell and I overheard them," she said. "They were making up after their spat on the train."

"Well, they can't be completely reconciled, because she's not with him," Robbie said.

Lindsey glanced at the stairwell door to see if Penny was coming. There was no sign of her. Lindsey wondered if she should go back out there and see if Penny was all right or let things be. Possibly, Penny's room was on the first floor and she'd left through the exit down there.

Lindsey decided to finish checking the second floor and then go down the stairwell and back to the first floor to her room. She started down the hallway, and Robbie fell into step beside her.

"I'm surprised you're still here," Lindsey said. "I thought Emma would have sent you home."

"The department is short on officers," he said. "She's got two of them, Kirkland and Wilcox, here, but the rest are dealing with the emergency calls from the blizzard and the search for—"

He stopped talking as if he didn't want to upset Lindsey.

She reached over and squeezed his arm, letting him know she appreciated the kindness. "It's okay. I know she has people out looking for Sully as well as the police boat and Coast Guard, and I wouldn't be surprised if she called in a favor with the state police as well. Between you and me, I thought if anyone could sniff him out, it would be Heathcliff."

"I understand, but just so you know, Kirkland and I searched every room," Robbie said. "If Sully was here, we would have found him."

Lindsey felt her shoulders slump. She hadn't realized she'd been holding so tightly to the hope that her husband was hidden here at the inn until it was taken away.

"I'm sorry," Robbie said. He gave her a half hug.

"And you're sure?" she asked.

"Positive," he said. "We both searched all the rooms from top to bottom, bathrooms and closets and under the beds. The basement here is quite terrifying, by the way."

A small huff of amusement slipped out of Lindsey. "I know."

"Come on, I'll walk you to your room. You need to get some sleep," he said.

"I can't imagine resting while he's out there missing," she protested.

"As the man who married you two lovebirds, I can assure you that if there is one thing I'm certain of, it's that Sully will find his way back to you come hell or high water, mark my words."

Lindsey nodded. She knew this to be true, but it was comforting to have it confirmed by a friend.

She used her key card to enter her room. Robbie came in with her and checked every nook and cranny before departing. He gave her another quick hug and a stern admonition to rest, closing the door behind him.

Lindsey glanced at Heathcliff, who had jumped up onto the bed, and at Zelda, who hadn't left her spot in Lindsey's coat. She took this as their way of telling her to take a beat and try to sleep. She trusted her furry friends to know best.

It didn't go well. She tossed and turned and then panicked when she did finally fall asleep only to wake up alone in a room she didn't recognize. She glanced at the side of the bed where her husband usually lay. Her heart sank.

Her phone rang, and she rolled to a seated position and grabbed it from the nightstand. She glanced at the name displayed. It was her boss, formerly her employee, Ms. Cole, who had recently been elected mayor of their shoreline village. Mayor Cole had been in the position for a few months now, and Lindsey was impressed with how well she was handling it.

"Lindsey, I'm glad I caught you before you left for work," Mayor Cole said. "I'm keeping all of the town offices closed today."

"Oh, okay," Lindsey said. She ran a hand over her face. "I'll let my staff know."

"Thank you," Mayor Cole said. "There's no need for anyone to be out in this snowmageddon when they have roofs to sweep off, driveways to clear and pipes to keep from freezing."

"Agreed," Lindsey said. She felt her spine relax. She hadn't thought about work, and she couldn't imagine having to go in when she had no idea where her husband was.

She felt her nerves ratchet up at the thought, and she took a calming breath.

"I'll let you know if the town council and I decide we need to stay closed tomorrow as well," Mayor Cole said.

"All right, I'll plan accordingly," Lindsey said. She hoped she sounded more professional than she felt.

"Is everything all right, Lindsey?" Mayor Cole asked. "You sound strained."

"I haven't had my coffee yet," Lindsey said. At least that was true. "I'm sure I'll perk up soon."

Mayor Cole was silent for a moment, and then a small laugh escaped her. "I see what you did there. Thanks. I needed the levity."

"No problem," Lindsey said. She didn't admit that the pun hadn't been intentional. She was barely functional because worry was consuming her, but Mayor Cole had enough to do without adding Lindsey's living nightmare to it.

"Be careful out there," Mayor Cole said. "Everything is coated in ice. Don't go anywhere if you don't have to."

"Got it." Lindsey ended the call. She fired off a text to her adult services librarian, asking her to inform the staff of the closure. She went to put her phone down, when it beeped with an incoming text message. She glanced at the display screen to see there was a message from an unknown number. Even a snow event didn't stop spam calls, she supposed. Unless it wasn't spam.

With shaking fingers, she opened the message. It was a photo but the resolution was blurry. She squinted trying to make it out, and then she pinched it and widened her fingers across the screen so that it enlarged. It was a plain room with a large-screen TV showing the local news from New Haven. There was the weather forecast, a big yellow sun with temperatures in the forties, and the date and time of when the photo was taken. It took a moment to register that the date was today and the time was from forty-five minutes ago.

Sitting on the floor in front of the TV, with his hands bound and tape across his mouth, was Sully.

CHAPTER

16

BRIAR CREEK
PUBLIC LIBRARY

A hhh!" Lindsey cried. She started to text him back asking where he was, as if the message were from Sully, but obviously he hadn't taken the picture of himself. Whoever had kidnapped him took the picture and she had no idea what to say or do.

Her fingers trembled as she deleted the word *where*. What was she supposed to write? Did she demand that they return her husband? Ask what they wanted? Threaten them with the police? That seemed like a bad idea. Frustration and fear made her shake, and Heathcliff crawled across the bed and pressed into her side as if sensing her inner turmoil.

Three dots appeared. The person was typing, probably because they'd seen Lindsey start typing. The message when it arrived was short and to the point.

**The book for him. Details to follow. No
police. I'm watching.**

A strangled cry sounded in Lindsey's throat. Sully was alive. She'd believed it to be true, but to have it confirmed broke through all her defenses, and she sobbed as a relief so powerful it almost knocked her out swept through her.

Not knowing what else to do, she texted, **Okay.** She wanted to call the number and beg and plead for the person to return Sully and that she'd do anything they asked, but she didn't. She put her phone down on the nightstand, put her face in her hands and wept. Sully was alive. She would see him again. Everything was going to be all right.

Heathcliff, as if sensing her distress, pressed his cold nose into her fingers, licking away the stream of relieved tears that fell from her eyes.

"Thanks, buddy," she said. She patted his head. A meow sounded, and she noticed that Zelda had left her spot in Lindsey's jacket and moved to her other side, settling against her hip.

She stroked the cat's head and received an immediate deep purr. She supposed she'd finally been forgiven, or maybe Zelda, too, was sympathetic to Lindsey's tears.

She rose from her seat on the bed. She hadn't changed her clothes, opting to sleep in her jeans and sweatshirt just in case something happened and she needed to be up and moving in moments. She slipped on her shoes, checking her phone constantly in case there was another message. She checked Sully's, too, but there was nothing. She wanted to be ready as soon as more instructions were sent. She would do anything. Trade anything . . . wait.

She sank back onto the bed. The message read *The book for him*. There was only one book the person could mean, and Lindsey no longer had possession of it. She had to get it back. She needed to have it in hand as soon as they demanded a swap. But how? Emma had locked the book in the vault at the police station. But the text message had also said *no police*.

How was Lindsey supposed to get the book back without the help of the police? She had to ask them for the book if it was going to be exchanged for Sully. How was she supposed to do this? Break into the jail? Steal the book? She had to assume that whoever had kidnapped Sully knew the police had the book and they expected Lindsey to get it for them.

She stared at her phone, willing the person to message her with more information. They said they were watching, but was it a hollow threat? Should she go to Emma anyway? Would they see her? What should she do? She looked at the picture of Sully again. She blew it up, studying it from every angle. It was no place she recognized.

She hopped up from the bed, pacing back and forth across the room. She needed to get out of here. She needed to be ready.

She crossed to the sliding glass doors and pulled the curtain back. A huge snowdrift was pressed up against them, but the sun was high and bright, and the sky was a clear deep blue, the blue of hope and optimism. The blizzard was over. Sully was alive. She'd focus on those two things and figure the rest out.

She decided her first order of business was to go home. She'd get the pets settled while she waited for further instructions. And while she waited, she'd figure out how to get her hands on the rare copy of *Strangers on a Train*.

She quickly fed the pets with the food she'd packed, and made herself a hot cup of coffee from the mini coffeepot in the room. She sipped carefully, holding her phone in one hand, not willing to put it down and risk missing a message. She did text Charlie asking him to come and get her and the pets as soon as possible. He texted back that he was on his way.

Lindsey packed up her crew and hustled them to the lobby to meet him. When she arrived, Michelle was staring out the large bay window that overlooked the parking lot and the surrounding trees. Lindsey joined her and felt her mouth slowly slide open.

"Mayor Cole was right. Everything is coated in ice," she observed. "Everything."

"Yeah, and check out the drifts," Michelle said. "They're about ten feet high."

As they watched, Charlie and his snowplow pulled into the parking lot. He stopped in front of the main door. The engine quit and he slowly climbed down, exhaustion in his every step. Lindsey felt bad for calling him when he had clearly been plowing all night, but she had no idea how else she could get home, and she had to go—now!—before

Emma turned up and asked questions that Lindsey wasn't prepared to answer.

"Charlie!" Lindsey cried as he stepped through the doors. "Are you all right?"

"Yeah, I'm good." He smiled. It was a tired one, but the usual Charlie Peyton spark was still in his eyes. "I caught a few hours of sleep when even espresso couldn't keep me awake."

"How's the town look?" Michelle asked.

"Like this." Charlie gestured outside. "Snowdrifts as high as houses, trees covered in ice, and the sunlight blindingly bright, reflecting off the pristine white snow. It's going to take a few days to dig out from this. The temperature is rising, but not enough to melt this much snow very fast."

"Any chance you could take me by the pier?" Lindsey asked. "I want to see if I can find Sully's truck."

"Sure, it's on the way," he said.

Lindsey turned to Michelle. "Thanks for letting me and the critters stay here."

"Anytime." Michelle picked up Zelda's carrier and followed Lindsey to the truck. Once Heathcliff and Lindsey's bag were settled in back, she clipped in the carrier. Zelda burrowed into the blanket, clearly not enjoying their excursion outside.

"If Emma asks for me, could you let her know I took my pets home?" Lindsey asked.

"Sure thing," Michelle said. "Between you and me, I'm hoping things wrap up with this investigation so I can go back to business as usual. Speaking of which, I need to go get the waffle iron loaded. The guests all seem to be sleeping in today, but when they wake up, I'm betting they'll be hungry."

"Waffles?" Charlie asked. "Blueberry?"

"Of course," Michelle said. She looked at his crestfallen face and said, "Come back and you can have all the waffles you want. I owe you for keeping me plowed out last night."

Charlie brightened up and said, "Come on, Lindsey, what are you waiting for?"

Lindsey shared a smile with Michelle and hopped into the truck. She checked her phone as she buckled her seat belt. No new message. She tried not to worry. She was leaving the inn. There was no chance that whoever had sent the message would see her talking to Emma or any of the other officers and get the wrong idea.

Charlie started the engine and they left the inn behind. As soon as he turned onto the street, he asked, "All right, what's going on?"

"You mean other than our town being blanketed in snow, the inn full of suspects in a potential murder on a train, and my husband missing?" she asked.

"Yeah, why are you in such a hurry to get home?" he asked. "I'd think you'd want to stay near Emma in case she learns something about Sully. Plus, there's a waffle machine, so what gives?"

"Nothing," Lindsey said. It came out too quick. She knew it as soon as she spoke, so she tried to sound calmer.

"I just want to get the pets home. I think if Sully is going to turn up on his own, it will be at home."

"That makes sense, I guess," Charlie said. He sounded doubtful, and Lindsey wished she could tell him what was really happening, but she couldn't risk it. She needed wheels, and she needed to figure out how to get the book back. She wanted to be ready when whoever had Sully offered the exchange.

They drove silently through the village, which looked like a ghost town. Absolutely no one was out and about. None of the residents had begun shoveling their driveways or using their snowblowers, and Lindsey wondered if the sheer amount of snow was so daunting that they were all taking a collective breath before they started what was going to be a very long day of digging out.

"Isn't this the spot where Sully usually parks?" Charlie asked.

The parking lot adjacent to the pier had already been plowed out. There was one midsize car parked in the corner, but the rest of the spaces were vacant, making it an easy cleanup for the plows that had come through.

Lindsey stared at the spot. There was no doubt about it. Sully's pickup truck was gone. She stared out the windshield as if she could manifest it out of thin air. No such luck.

"Looks like whoever took Sully used his own truck to do it," Charlie said. "We should call that into Emma. It might give her a lead."

"Right," Lindsey said. "Good idea. I'll call on the ride."

Charlie left the parking lot and headed through town to the neighborhood where Lindsey and Sully's small cottage was nestled with others just like it. Originally summer homes, they'd been remodeled for year-round residency. They were snug and cozy, built right along the water, and Lindsey couldn't imagine living anywhere else.

She pulled Emma up in her contacts and pressed "Call." Surely, phoning in her husband's missing truck wouldn't be considered the same as reporting the photo and message she'd gotten, and how could the person who had Sully even know that she was calling Emma? She refused to be paranoid. Besides, it would be impossible to explain to Charlie why she didn't call in Sully's missing truck.

"Where are you, Lindsey?" Emma answered without a greeting. "I stopped by your room but it was empty."

"I'm with Charlie," Lindsey said. "The pets needed to get home."

"Of course. And you're all right?" Emma asked.

"I'm fine," Lindsey answered. Her voice came out higher than usual and she cleared her throat. "But we did stop by the pier to see if Sully's truck was there, and it wasn't."

"How could you tell with all this snow?"

"The pier parking lot has been plowed," Lindsey said. "There's only one car there, and it isn't Sully's."

"So whoever took him took his truck, too," Emma said. "Meaning they didn't have wheels, because they found themselves staying in town unexpectedly. I'll put out an

APB on Sully's truck. Can you text me the make, model and license plate number?"

"Doing it now," Lindsey said. She opened the text app while they talked and sent Emma the information. "Did you figure out Andrew Shields's real occupation?"

"Oh yes," Emma said. "You're going to love this. He's a private eye."

"A private investigator?" Lindsey asked. "Who is he working for?"

"He won't say, but it definitely has to do with that archivist conference," Emma said. "And I'd bet my hat it has to do with that volume of *Strangers on a Train*. It's already tied to one murder. I'd like to clear this up so it isn't tied to any more."

Lindsey shivered. She didn't like this. Not one little bit. The thought that Sully could be in jeopardy like Henry if she didn't retrieve the book and make the trade made her heart race and her palms sweat.

"Speaking of the book," Lindsey said. "You locked it in the vault at the police station, right?"

"Yes, Kirkland delivered it there yesterday," Emma said. "Unfortunately, most of the state will be digging out all day today and tomorrow, and the earliest the crime scene investigators can get down here is the day after that. My hope is that there's some DNA evidence on the book that will reveal the killer and tie it to the murder of Henry Standish."

"Is there any timeline on how long that might take?" Lindsey asked. She didn't even bother mentioning getting an archivist to oversee the examination of the book. She'd worry about that when Sully was returned.

"I'll ask for a rush, but it really depends on who is juggling the highest-profile case," Emma said. "Sad but true."

"How high profile is this one?" Lindsey asked.

"Not very," Emma admitted. "Outside of his own archivist world, Henry Standish was just a book nerd who met an unfortunate end on a train, and he's a resident of New York, so I can't even use the 'but the victim is local' leverage."

Lindsey hadn't known Henry well, and even though he'd had some sketchy stuff go down with his previous job, she still felt that he should be remembered better than that. She sighed.

"Any news on Sully?" Lindsey asked.

Emma was quiet for a beat. "I'm sorry. No."

Lindsey nodded. She had so been hoping that Emma had gotten a ransom note, too. But with the book locked up at the station, the ransom text on her phone, and the kidnapper's explicit instructions not to go to the police, she said nothing.

"Let me know if anyone spots Sully's truck," she said.

"Will do. Keep in touch and be careful," Emma said. "And I know it's difficult, but try to keep a positive outlook. Sully was a Navy SEAL. He can handle himself."

In that moment the temptation to tell Emma everything was so strong, Lindsey had to actually bite her tongue. She couldn't risk Sully's life; she wouldn't risk it on a gamble that could go horribly wrong. She was going to follow her instincts, and at the moment, they told her to get the book back and be ready.

Of course, the problem was that she couldn't get the book. There was simply no way. Whoever had Sully had to be the person who planted the book in her belongings in the chaotic aftermath of Henry's body being discovered. It was clear they thought she had access to the book, so either they knew she was friends with the chief of police or they didn't know she'd turned the book over. They obviously had no idea how complicated this was, but maybe that could work to her advantage. The thought gave her a tiny sliver of hope no bigger than the last phase of the moon before it disappeared, but it was all she had.

She and Charlie arrived at her house and unloaded the pets, letting Heathcliff patrol the yard while Zelda went back to her radiator. The house was locked up nice and tight, although Charlie insisted on inspecting every inch of it for her protection. She kept her phone in her hand, waiting for the next text or call, but there was none.

Charlie had to leave to finish plowing the town out. Lindsey waved to him from the porch, willing him to move along. *Hurry up. Faster. Go. Go. Go.* When his taillights had finally disappeared, she grabbed her backpack and threw some supplies in it, including her own conference tote bag, which she'd packed in her carry-on.

She checked the house one more time, patted Zelda and Heathcliff and told him to be a good watchdog. Then she hurried to their small detached garage. She struggled through the snowdrifts until she reached the side door. She pushed it open and fell inside. Her bike was parked in its usual spot, and she hefted it up, hauling it outside. She had an idea. It was a long shot but it was the only way she could think of to try to outsmart whoever had texted her with the picture of Sully.

She closed the garage door and wheeled her bike out to the street. When Lindsey had moved to Briar Creek several years ago, she had promised herself she would be more environmentally conscious, and so she didn't own a car. She'd ridden her bike to and from work for the first couple of years she'd lived here, and now she and Sully shared his truck, but she still biked to work most days, even in the winter.

She climbed on, fastening her helmet. Since it had been in the basket of the bike, it was cold, and she felt as if it were freezing her skull. She shivered, willing her body heat to warm it up. She tightened her scarf about her neck, zipped her jacket all the way up, and made certain that no frigid air could seep in between her gloves and her sleeves. She put her backpack in the basket, hoping if anyone was watching they'd be fooled into thinking she had the book.

Pushing off with her right foot, she set off. The snowplows had done an excellent job, considering the amount of snow they'd been trying to move. She couldn't see the sidewalk, and there was still some hard-packed snow that the plows hadn't been able to remove, so she stayed on the pavement visible in the deep grooves made by the tires of the plows that had been working all night long.

There were more people out now than earlier, and she

waved to a few of her neighbors, although she didn't stop to chat. She was hoping they'd think she was going to work and leave her be. She didn't want to have to explain anything, especially since her first stop was the police station.

She set her bike against the side of the building, since the bike rack was buried in snow. She grabbed her backpack and made a show of pulling it onto her shoulders on the off chance that the person who said they were watching was actually doing just that.

Pulling the glass door open, she strode inside. She wasn't cold because she'd warmed up while pedaling her bike, so she was relieved to pull off her helmet and loosen her scarf.

"Lindsey, what are you doing here?" Molly Hatcher asked. She was the police station's administrative assistant and dispatcher. A robust brunette with a ready laugh, she was about as unflappable as a person could be without being in a coma.

"I was just passing by and wondered if Emma was in," Lindsey said. It sounded lame even to her, but Molly didn't seem to think so.

"No, she's at the inn and has been ever since they brought the train passengers over there," she said. She waved her hands at her desk, indicating her phone and computer. "It's been a madhouse in this storm. We've had people calling us about mailboxes that were plowed over, frozen pipes and even a complaint about a late pizza delivery. I'm sorry. When did we get into the plowing, pipes and pizza business?"

Lindsey knew that while bad weather frequently brought

out the best in people, the opposite was true as well. "Maybe things will settle down now that the sun is out."

"I hope so. Detective Trimble just stopped by. He said there's a lot of pressure coming down from the higher-ups to solve the murder because the train company doesn't want the bad press."

"They think people will be afraid to ride the train because they might get murdered?" Lindsey asked. "That makes no sense."

Molly shrugged.

"Do you happen to know if he took the book that Emma had Kirkland lock up in the vault?" Lindsey asked.

"No, he didn't," Molly said. "He'd have to ask me to get it for him as I'm the only one besides Emma who knows the combination."

"Which would be?" Lindsey asked.

Molly stared at her for a beat and then threw her head back and laughed. It was an infectious sound that always made Lindsey laugh, too, but not today. Today she felt as if she were made of glass shards haphazardly taped together that might fall apart at the slightest disturbance.

Glancing at her face, Molly stopped laughing. "I'm so sorry. I can't believe I forgot what you're going through. Come here."

Lindsey would have refused, but when Molly got it in her head that she was going to hug you, it was best to just give in. Not surprisingly, Molly's hug comforted her a bit, and when Molly released her, she felt steadier than she had since she'd gotten that text this morning.

"Sully's going to be okay," Molly said. She stated it with such assurance that Lindsey almost asked for her help, but she didn't. She knew she couldn't put Molly in the position of committing a crime. She had to hope that just being here, popping in, was enough.

"Thanks, Moll," she said. "I'd better go. I'm trying to keep busy and figured I'd check on the library."

"Good idea," Molly said. "Do you want me to tell the chief you were looking for her?"

"No, I was just, you know, killing time," Lindsey said.

Molly nodded, looking sympathetic. Lindsey left the station and retrieved her bike.

She crossed Main Street, looped around to the back of the library building and found the parking lot was clear of snow. *Thank you, Charlie!* She parked her bike at the back entrance and hurried inside, shutting the library's alarm off by using the keypad beside the door.

The building was dark, which, given that Mayor Cole had said she was keeping the town's departments closed, was not a big surprise. Still, Lindsey wanted to check on the building and make certain there were no indications of burst pipes or heating issues.

She flicked on the lights as she walked through. Just the smell of the books soothed her. Everything was going to be okay. She had an inkling of a plan, and she was hopeful that she could make it work. She went right to her office and took the set of keys she kept there out of her desk.

Walking down the hallway to the storage room used by the Friends of the Library for their book sale, she hoped against hope that they had what she needed. She wondered if she should call the crafternooners for help. Lindsey was not the craftiest of the bunch, and this was going to take some skill to pull it off.

She took her phone out of her pocket and sent a quick text to the crafternooners group chat. She didn't want anyone to get hurt trying to navigate the icy storms, but if they could advise her over the phone with her project, it might make all the difference.

She put her phone back in her pocket, where she would feel it vibrate if she received another text, then unlocked the storage room door and entered the musty space, flicking on the overhead lights as she went. The library received hundreds of books as donations every year and, as a fund-raiser, the Friends of the Library held an annual book sale in the spring, selling the ones that were in good enough shape to be rehomed. Lindsey was given first dibs on the incoming books, however, so that she could fill in any gaps in the library's collection.

She was positive, almost one hundred percent, that the library had been gifted a copy of *Strangers on a Train* that they hadn't needed. She just hoped it hadn't been sold yet.

Lindsey approached the steel shelves, pleased to see that the books were sorted alphabetically by author. She'd know in moments if her plan was going to work or not. She went right to the *H*'s. She scanned the spines—Hammett, Hemingway—until she reached *Hi*. Hiaasen. Higgins. Highsmith! She glanced at the title. *Strangers on a Train*. Yes!

CHAPTER

17

BRIAR CREEK
PUBLIC LIBRARY

Lindsey examined the book. It was clothbound, it didn't smell like mold or cigarette smoke, and the pages were clean, not tattered or crumbling. She looked at the title page. It looked like the one from the conference minus the inscription. She could work with this. She tucked the book under her arm and left the storage closet.

She checked her phone for what felt like the thousandth time. There was no message. If she didn't have the original sitting right there, she'd think she imagined the entire thing. She took a screenshot of the picture of Sully and the message just in case she accidentally deleted them. She took a moment to zoom in on Sully's face. His bright blue eyes were squinted, and his chin was tipped up in defiance. She knew that expression. Her husband was furious. She hoped he still was. She traced his features with her index finger. She had to believe that he was and that he'd fight to survive. Any other outcome was unacceptable.

She went into the workroom, which led to her office. She flicked on the light switch beside the door. She had no idea how she was going to do what needed doing, and she felt the stirrings of panic in her belly.

"Hello!" a chipper voice called from out in the main part of the library.

Lindsey put the book on her desk and hurried forward. At the inn, she'd texted her adult services librarian, Ann Marie, and had her call the rest of the staff to let them know the building would stay closed for the day. She wondered if Ann Marie had forgotten to make the calls. She was the mother of two rambunctious preteen boys, so it would be understandable.

She stepped into the area behind the checkout desk and found Paula Turner, who had been recently promoted to the head of circulation in Mayor Cole's place, and the craftiest of her crafternooner friends, standing there.

"Paula, what are you doing here? Did Ann Marie call you about the library staying closed?"

"She did, but then I got your message about needing craft advice and I thought I'd come over instead of trying to help through texts. Crafting really is a hands-on sort of thing," Paula said. "Besides, Hannah and I were just down the street, helping to shovel the church's walkway, so I figured I'd pop in over here."

"Because anything is better than shoveling snow?" Lindsey asked.

Paula grinned. "Something like that. Hannah stayed to help sweep off the church roof, but I don't like heights, so . . ."

A knock on the front door sounded, and Lindsey glanced over to see Violet and Nancy standing there with Beth.

"Looks like I'm not the only one who got tired of shoveling," Paula said. "I'll let them in."

"I'll make some coffee," Lindsey said. She turned and went to the break room, taking the opportunity to think about what she was about to ask her friends to do. She took out her phone and glanced at the picture of her husband. She had no choice. It really was that simple.

et me get this straight," Violet said. She cradled her coffee in her hands and blew across the surface, encouraging it to cool. "We're trying to commit forgery?"

"Partially," Lindsey said. She'd printed out the photo she'd taken of the title page of the original volume of *Strangers on a Train* when she and Sully had found the book at the conference. She had explained to her friends that she needed to make a replica of the book that was currently locked up in the police station. She hadn't explained why, wanting to keep them out of it as much as she could. She'd received considering looks from each of them, but then they seemed to come to a consensus.

Paula had been tasked with re-creating the book jacket, which entailed a lot of searching on the internet and attempting to print the right size on the printer. So far she hadn't been able to get the size exact, and the quality of the print left a lot to be desired as well. When Lindsey passed Paula's desk, she saw her hunched over her computer using a photo-editing program that made her swear like a sailor and threaten the program with physical harm.

Violet and Nancy were working on searching the internet for samples of Hitchcock's handwriting. Specifically, any notes he'd written in the margins of books, like the ones Lindsey had seen in the Highsmith volume. She wanted to make this book as close to the one that the police had as possible. She had no idea how the person who'd texted her planned to make the exchange, but she wanted to be prepared.

"I'm still not clear on why we're doing this," Beth said. She was in her office, using her art skills to try to match the handwriting of Alfred Hitchcock and Patricia Highsmith, and while she was close, it was still clear to Lindsey that it was a forgery. "If this is for a display, you really are going above and beyond."

"It's not for a display, but it is very, very important," Lindsey said. She could hear the anxiety in her voice, and Beth glanced at her. She slowly put her pen down and pushed the practice sheet away from her.

"Lindsey, I'm your best friend," Beth said. "Tell me what's going on."

"I don't want you pulled into this any more than you already are," Lindsey said.

"You have me practicing the signatures of two dead

people," Beth said. "How much farther in can I possibly get?"

"Fair point," Lindsey agreed. She glanced over her shoulder at the others. She stepped into Beth's office and closed the door behind her. She took her phone out of her pocket and opened the messages app. She then handed it to Beth. "I received that this morning."

Beth frowned and took the phone. As soon as she read the words and saw the picture, she gasped. "That's Sully. Someone has Sully."

"Shhh," Lindsey hushed her. She glanced over her shoulder through the office window and into the break room. Violet and Nancy were chatting while looking at a computer screen. Paula was muttering as she held up another printout against the copy of the book Lindsey had found.

"Sorry, but this is huge," Beth said. "Have you talked to Emma? Has she seen this? Did you tell his parents?"

"No, no and no," Lindsey said. She winced. "The text specifically says 'no police' and that they're watching. I can't risk it."

"Oh, Lindsey." Beth shook her head. "You have to tell Emma. She's not just the chief of police, she's our friend. She'd help us."

Lindsey took her phone back and put it in her pocket. "The message said 'no police.'"

"But can't they track the phone number?"

"I tried a phone number reverse search," Lindsey said. "I think it's a burner phone, which makes it impossible to trace without a search warrant to the phone provider. We don't have that kind of time."

"I still think—" Beth began, but Lindsey interrupted.

"What if it was Aidan?" Lindsey asked. "What would you do if someone took him and said 'no police' and you knew that they'd already killed a person?"

Beth stared at her. The expression on her face said it all. "I'd do the same thing you're doing. I'm sorry. I'm just panicking."

"I know the feeling," Lindsey said.

"Any clue as to where they're holding him?" Beth asked.

Lindsey shook her head. "I don't recognize the room he's in. It's a big-screen TV and him. That's it. There's nothing on the white walls or tile floor to indicate where this is." She tapped the phone's screen. "I thought he might be at the inn, assuming it's one of the passengers who took him. Where else could they hold him? But Robbie searched it and I took Heathcliff all over the building and no luck."

"At least we know he's safe," Beth said. She rose from her seat, circled the desk and hugged Lindsey. "We'll get him back."

Lindsey clung to her friend, surprised by how desperately she'd needed to tell someone what was happening. She felt her phone buzz in her pocket at the same time that the incoming message chime sounded. She broke the hug and stepped back. Beth looked at her with wide eyes. Lindsey took a deep breath and glanced at the display. It was the same unknown number that had texted her before.

She opened the message.

**One hour. Boat tour office. Come alone.**
**Bring the book.**

"We have one hour," she said.

"All right, let's do this." Beth nodded. She sounded breathless, and Lindsey knew that Beth was just as nervous as she was.

She squeezed her friend's shoulder, more grateful than she could say. She went back out to see if she could help the others. To get to the pier in time, she needed to leave five minutes before the designated time. That gave them fifty-five minutes to try to replicate the coveted book.

She closed her eyes, thinking of Sully, and she knew they'd get it done. They had no other option.

"I think I've got it," Paula announced. "I went into my editing program and set the perspective to—never mind, who cares? The point is, I got the cover the right size, and I think if I can manipulate the color on the digital printout by using the copy machine, and run a two-sided print so that the inside flaps actually have the description, we may have a winner."

Lindsey felt her knees sag in relief. "Excellent."

The cover and the title page were the most important things. If the person holding Sully looked at the copyright page first and discovered it was a later edition, they were doomed, but she couldn't worry about that right now.

"We have several examples of Hitchcock's margin notes," Violet said. "Should we deliver them to Beth to practice?"

"Yes, please," Lindsey said. "Not to pressure anyone, but I need to have all of this done in less than an hour."

Paula looked at her and said, "Is that when the person holding Sully wants to make the swap?"

Lindsey blinked right as Nancy cried, "I knew it!"

"You did," Violet said.

"What? How?" Lindsey asked.

"Really? Why else would you try to replicate a book that we all know the chief has locked up in the station?" Nancy asked. "When did they contact you?"

"And how?" Paula asked.

"They sent me a text message with a picture of Sully tied up," Lindsey said. "They told me they wanted to swap him for the book, so I assumed they believed that I had access to the book at the police department, which was why I stopped there earlier. They also said not to contact the police, so I didn't."

Lindsey glanced at their faces, looking for disapproval. There was none. Just compassion.

"Where are you meeting them?"

"Sully's office on the pier," she said. She glanced at the phone. "In fifty minutes."

"Let's do this!" Paula declared.

Lindsey took the samples of writing that Nancy and Violet had found and delivered them with the book to Beth in her office.

Paula finished the cover and joined the others while they waited for Beth to finish with the book. When the door opened, they had ten minutes until the designated meeting time. Beth handed the book to Lindsey. "I never thought all of my art classes would lead to this, but I think it's a darn good fake."

Lindsey opened the book and checked the title page. She opened the photos on her phone and found the picture of the original book's title page. Beth had done it. Highsmith's note to Hitchcock was spot-on.

"This is amazing," Lindsey said. "I can't tell the difference from the original at all."

Beth smiled.

"All right," Paula said. "It's time for the cover."

Lindsey handed her the book, and Paula carefully placed it in the paper cover she'd made. She breathed a sigh of relief as everything matched up perfectly. She handed it back to Lindsey and said, "Go get him."

Lindsey studied the book in her hand. Paula had managed to age the cover just enough to pass a cursory examination. It was Lindsey's dearest hope that the person she was making the exchange with was in a hurry and wouldn't examine the book too closely. Between the short notice and the blizzard, they'd never believe Lindsey could pull off a duplicate, so if they got very lucky, it should work just long enough for her to get Sully out of there.

"All right," she said. "Wish me luck."

She put the book inside the conference tote bag she'd brought in her backpack. Again, Lindsey hoped that the person who had Sully believed it was the one they'd tucked into her luggage. She pulled on her coat, hat, scarf and gloves and tucked the book bag under her arm.

"Do you want us to come with you?" Beth asked. "We could follow at a distance."

"Thanks for offering," Lindsey said. "But they said I was to go alone, and I'm in too deep not to do what they've asked. Stay here. I'll have my phone with me."

"Be careful," Nancy said.

"If you get a weird feeling, get out of there," Violet added.

"She's right," Paula said. "Do not let them grab you, too."

Lindsey hadn't thought of that. She nodded slowly, trying to wrap her mind around being in a hostage-ransom situation. This was the stuff of books and movies, not real life, except it was very much her life.

"I'll be right back," Lindsey said. "With Sully."

She left the library through the back door. She debated taking her bike but decided against it. There were even more people out and about, cleaning up after the blizzard, and the streets were clearer than they'd been a few hours ago. She walked briskly down the sidewalk, afraid of being late, and arrived at the parking lot where Sully's truck should have been. There was still no sign of it. If the person who had grabbed him had taken his truck, wouldn't they have brought him back to the pier the same way? Unless they knew that the police would be looking for the truck.

Lindsey approached the pier, which was also covered in snow. The Blue Anchor restaurant sat at the base. Its windows were dark, and she knew that Mary and Ian had likely remained closed while they awaited word about Sully's whereabouts. She wondered if she should have called them to help her, but she didn't want to risk it. They had a little girl to take care of, and Lindsey knew Sully wouldn't want any of them put in danger.

She passed by the restaurant and headed down the thick wooden planks covered in snow. The tiny office that Sully, Ian and Ronnie worked out of was also dark. Again, Lindsey felt a pang of conscience as she hadn't gotten in touch with Ronnie about Sully's whereabouts either. She had a key to his office, and as a cold wind blew in from the water, she decided she'd wait in there.

She pulled off her glove and unlocked the door. She pulled the door open and stepped inside, relieved to be out of the chilly air. She flicked on the lights and glanced at the clock on the wall beside Ronnie's desk. She had three minutes to go. She sat down on the edge of one of the chairs, clutching the book bag in her hands.

How would this go down? Would they demand the book first? What if they examined it and discovered it was a fake? They might murder both Sully and her. She felt her heart pound hard in her chest. She needed some kind of leverage. She needed to make certain that she got Sully before they looked too closely at the book.

She glanced around the office. There wasn't much to use as a weapon. A stapler? A coffee mug? Sticky notes? Somehow she didn't think the threat of a paper cut would sway them. In fact, there was no way she'd be able to threaten them with bodily harm when they could just stab or shoot Sully. No, she had to force their hand by putting what they wanted in jeopardy.

Lindsey hopped up from her seat. She hurried over to the kitchenette. Sure enough, in the junk drawer, she found what she was looking for. She tucked it into her sleeve and sat back down. She could hear the second hand on the clock ticking. She felt as if it were moving backward. At last, she heard footsteps on the pier outside. She glanced through the window and saw two figures coming her way.

One was Sully! She'd recognize his long-legged gait anywhere. The other one . . . She squinted as they drew closer. Recognition hit as they reached the door. She gasped. The other one was the person in black that she'd seen on the train.

CHAPTER

18

BRIAR CREEK
PUBLIC LIBRARY

The door was pulled open, and Sully was shoved inside. He stumbled across the threshold, catching himself before he fell.

"Sully!" Lindsey hopped up from her seat. She could see that his hands were still bound, and he had a wide piece of tape across his mouth. His bright blue gaze found hers, and his eyes went soft with concern and worry for her well-being.

"I'm okay," she said. She was about to step forward, but the person in black yanked Sully back by his arm.

They kept one hand in their pocket and leaned toward Sully. Their voice was a deep growl, and it was clear they were disguising it when they said, "Don't forget my warning. I will shoot her if you give me reason to."

Lindsey felt her breath hitch. Okay, so that's how it was

going to be. She worked the sleeve of her coat until she felt her weapon of choice fall into her palm. She cupped it, keeping it hidden.

"Give me the book," the person said. Lindsey tried to make out anything that might identify them, but much like on the train, she couldn't see anything distinguishing. They wore a long black wool coat, black jeans, plain black boots, a black hat, a black scarf that covered their face from the nose down and a pair of black sunglasses, which was new, but she'd never seen their eyes clearly before anyway.

"Let him go first," Lindsey said. Her voice came out high and wobbly. She cleared her throat. She had so wanted to have the control in this situation.

"Did you not hear what I said?" the person in black asked. They waved the hand in the pocket of their coat. "I will shoot you if you don't give me the book right now."

Lindsey took the book out of the bag and held it up in front of her. Then she flicked the lighter in her other hand, holding the flame just under the book. "Did you not hear me? I said let him go now or I'll turn this book to ash."

She didn't take her eyes off her adversary, but she saw Sully stiffen out of the corner of her eye. She could only imagine how wild-eyed she looked at the moment. She hadn't known it was possible to feel the level of terror-rage she had pumping through her system. This person was threatening her husband. They were darn lucky she didn't charge over there and rip them limb from limb.

"All right! Fine!" the person snapped. They shoved Sully across the floor. He staggered and looked as if he'd strike back. His captor jammed the gun in their pocket into his back. "First I shoot her, then you."

Sully quit fighting. The person pushed him into the back office and closed the door. "Give me the book and you can go to him."

"Take your hand out of your coat first," Lindsey said. She watched as they began to move. She raised the flame closer to the book. "Slowly."

The person lifted a black-gloved hand out of their pocket. They weren't holding a gun, obviously leaving it in their coat. Thank goodness. Lindsey circled them, keeping them in sight as she moved toward the table. She released the flame on the lighter and snatched up the tote bag. She dropped the book inside. When the person would have stepped forward to take it, she held up the lighter and the bag. They stopped and held their hands out at their sides.

"I don't want to hurt you. I just want the book."

"Really?" Lindsey asked. She thought about the past day she'd spent petrified that her husband was dead, fearing she'd never see him again. She lunged toward them, forcing them back as she moved toward the door. "Because you did a hell of a job."

She pushed the door open and threw the book out into a snowdrift as hard as she could.

"Ah!" the person in black cried as they shoved past her and dashed outside to retrieve the book. "You b—"

Their words were cut off when Lindsey yanked the door shut and turned the dead bolt.

She didn't wait to see if they found the book in the massive

snowdrift, but ran into Sully's office. She found him trying to cut his hands loose from the zip ties with a pair of
scissors. She grabbed the scissors and snipped the thick
plastic. Then she reached up and ripped the tape off his
mouth.

That was as far as she got in examining him when he
scooped her into his arms and held her in a crusher hug. He
planted a kiss on her lips and cupped her face. "Are you all
right? Did they hurt you?"

"No, I'm fine," she said.

He closed his eyes for just a second as if the relief at her
statement overwhelmed him. Then he stepped around her
and into the main office, looking for the person in black.
"Where are they? What happened?"

Lindsey pointed to the window. "I threw the book into
a snowdrift."

Sully looked from her to the window, where he could see
the person in black frantically trying to shovel through the
snow with their hands, and then back at her. His lips ticked
up in one corner and he said, "Wait here."

"No," she said. "Don't you dare go out there."

Sully was already unlocking the door. He got one step
outside into the cold when three police officers appeared.

"Don't move!" Emma shouted. She pointed her gun at
the person in black, who sank back onto their heels, looking utterly defeated. "Hands on your head!"

The person scanned the area as if looking for an escape.
Unless they planned to jump off the pier into the bay, there
was none. They slowly raised their hands to their head.

"Emma, check for a gun in their left coat pocket," Sully said.

Emma gave a curt nod. Once Officer Kirkland had their hands secured behind their back, she reached into the coat pocket and came out with a screwdriver.

Sully muttered an epithet under his breath, but Lindsey felt nothing but relief. Whoever this person was, they wouldn't actually have killed them—unless they were very handy with that screwdriver, which she supposed they could be, but it seemed unlikely.

"The book!" the person in black cried. Their voice was no longer a deep disguised growl that Lindsey was certain she'd hear in her nightmares. Rather, it was a normal male voice, and it sounded familiar. Very familiar.

"You don't have to worry about it, Kirk," she said. "It was a fake."

Emma reached out and took the sunglasses off his face and then the hat. Sure enough, Kirk Duncan was the person in black. Lindsey supposed it made sense, and it proved what Henry had accused him of, being obsessed with the book, but Lindsey found it deeply disappointing. She had actually believed him when he professed to care about Penny.

"This looks bad, but I can explain," he said. "I wasn't going to hurt anyone. I just wanted the book."

"I don't think Henry Standish would agree that your intent wasn't to cause harm," Emma said. One eyebrow ticked up as she stared at him, her face impassive.

"I had nothing to do with that," Kirk insisted. "The

book belongs to my grandmother, and I was merely trying to get it back for her."

"You can explain down at the station," Emma said. She gestured for Officer Kirkland to lead the way with Kirk. She turned to face Lindsey and Sully. "You're coming, too. I need your statements."

"How did you know we were here?" Lindsey asked.

"Penny Minton," Emma said. "She told me she saw Kirk sneaking out of the inn after breakfast. He was wearing a long black coat, and she had heard that Lydia saw someone dressed like that in her room, so Penny suspected Kirk was up to something. Looks like she was right."

Lindsey remembered running into Kirk in the hallway the night before. He hadn't been wearing this black coat. She would have noticed. Instead, he'd been in a blue puffy coat. So where had this one come from?

She remembered his conversation with Penny from the stairwell and had assumed they were getting back together, but maybe Penny wasn't as easily taken in as Kirk had hoped.

Why had Kirk kidnapped Sully? Did he really think Lindsey had that much sway with the police department that she could get the book out of the vault? He must have seen her hand it over to Emma when she and Robbie interrupted their meeting at the inn.

How could Kirk not have understood how impossible his request was? Then she remembered his highly privileged life as the grandson of Jasmine Bellamy. It was a different world that he inhabited. He was likely used to getting what he wanted when he wanted it, and assumed the world worked the same way for everyone else. Well, it didn't.

They started to follow Officer Kirkland, but Lindsey stopped and said, "Give me a sec."

She hurried over to the snowdrift and began to dig just to the left of where Kirk had been tossing the snow. In a couple of feet, she found the hole the book had made when it flew into the snowbank. She pulled it out and hurried to follow them.

Emma glanced from the bag to Lindsey and said, "A fake, huh?"

"Yeah, we worked really hard on it," Lindsey said. "I had to pull in the crafternooners since I couldn't get my hands on the real book, and arts and crafts is not really my thing."

"You might have had the real book if you'd bothered to tell me what was happening," Emma said.

"Kirk very specifically said no police."

Emma muttered and shook her head. Her expression was one of peak peeved. "So, you take orders from a rando bad guy on a cell phone but not from me. Do I have that right?"

"If you kidnapped my husband, I would do what you said," Lindsey countered.

"I'll keep that in mind," Emma said.

"Whoa, whoa, whoa," Sully said. He moved so that he was walking in between the two of them. "No more kidnappings. I did not enjoy any of that."

"Do you know where he kept you?" Emma asked.

Sully shook his head. "Not for certain. He clocked me on the head when I was on the pier, and the next thing I knew, I was waking up in a room with a couch and a television, and that was it. The windows were covered and I couldn't see out, but I could hear the wind, and I thought I heard water, so I assumed I was near the beach. It wasn't until he put me in a boat this morning that I knew I'd been on one of the islands."

"One of the islands?" Lindsey repeated. That possibility had never occurred to her.

"Was there anyone with you, keeping watch?" Emma asked.

"Not that I know of. I was tied to the couch, so I couldn't really move. The few times he showed up to give me food and water and let me use the bathroom, he indicated he had a gun, so I bided my time, figuring I'd get a chance to escape eventually."

"But you had no idea that all of this was an exchange for the book?" Emma asked.

Sully shook his head. "He never spoke, and he was very careful to stay out of reach." He glanced up ahead to where Officer Kirkland was helping Kirk cross the street. He squinted at the other man's back. "The whole thing was surreal."

Lindsey squeezed his hand with hers. She felt the exact same way. As much of a book lover as she was, she couldn't imagine going to these lengths just to acquire a book. Maybe when Kirk confessed all, she'd understand, but at the moment, no.

They crossed the street and entered the police station. Molly was seated at the front desk. She took one look at Sully and sagged against her chair, put her hand on her chest and cried, "Oh, thank goodness."

"Hi, Moll." Sully smiled at her. "You all right?"

"Do you have any idea how worried we've all been? Ever since Ian found your boat without you in it, the entire town has been in a tizzy." She hurried around the desk and caught him in a hug that crushed.

"Found my boat?" Sully asked. He looked at Lindsey over Molly's head.

"Kirk cut it loose when he took off with you," Lindsey said. "Ian found it in the shallows."

Sully's face darkened with his rarely witnessed temper. He took a steadying breath. "Boat's okay?"

"Perfect condition," Lindsey assured him.

Molly let him go and said, "I'm so glad you're back and you're all right. Now, I have calls to make."

Lindsey reached for her own phone. "She's right. I need to call your parents and sister and let them know you're okay. When your boat was found without you in it, well, I think we all aged about ten years."

"Oh, darling, you should know I'd never leave you without a fight," he said. He hugged her close, and Lindsey felt everyone watching them, making matching *aw* expressions. She didn't care. She hugged him back, letting her gratitude that he was here and he was fine fill her from top to bottom.

She called her in-laws and handed the phone to Sully. They were delighted to hear their son's voice on the line. His mother cried, and Lindsey suspected his father did, too. He promised to be out to their island to visit them the next day, which eased their anxiety. He then used Lindsey's phone to call his sister and her husband. After that, Lindsey called Beth, who shrieked with delight, relieved that their plan had worked. Lindsey heard Nancy, Violet and Paula in the background, whooping when Beth relayed the good news.

Lindsey forwarded the text messages she'd received from Kirk to Emma and handed over the fake book that she and the crafternooners had created. Emma said nothing, and Lindsey couldn't gauge how irritated she was. She knew Emma had to be annoyed, but Lindsey was hoping the evidence she handed her would make Emma forgive her sooner rather than later.

"Thanks for the texts," Emma said. "That gives me something to question our kidnapper with." She led them to the break room, where the coffee was freshly brewed and there was a bin of cookies on the counter. "Help yourselves. Nancy dropped off the cookies this morning. Oatmeal raisin, the first line of defense against blizzard conditions, apparently."

"Thank you," Lindsey said. She noted she was ravenous, and Sully was already at the bin, grabbing a cookie while he poured them two cups of coffee.

"I'm going to question our suspect," Emma said. "Is there anything I should know before I begin?"

"Such as?" Sully asked through a bite of cookie. He took another and handed it to Lindsey.

"Do you think he was operating alone?"

"As I mentioned, no one else was there," Sully said. "He was alone when he caught me boarding my boat and sucker punched me."

"He's not that big of a guy," Emma said. "How did he haul you onto his boat without anyone noticing?"

"Since I was unconscious, I really can't say for certain," Sully said. "But he motored up beside my dock when I was prepping to go out, and asked me about the weather. I went to show him the forecast on my phone, and the next thing I knew I woke up tied to a sofa. He must have knocked me out and let me tumble right into his boat. It would certainly explain the pain in my hips and shoulder."

"Any idea which island? There are over a hundred out there, if you count the rocks," Emma said. She looked as if he'd just handed her the middle piece of a jigsaw puzzle with no picture to work from.

"No idea," Sully said. "Other than the picture he took to text to Lindsey, I was blindfolded the entire time, even on the ride back this morning. All I know is that it had to be one of the cottages with electricity and heat, otherwise I would have frozen to death in that storm."

"So he must have dumped you on the island and then come back and stolen your truck, which we haven't found yet, and gotten back to the inn without anyone noticing." Lindsey looked at Emma and asked, "Is that possible?"

"We have over forty people in that inn," Emma said. "I don't like it, but I suppose it's possible." She looked supremely annoyed.

"Wait, he took my truck?" Sully asked. Lindsey nodded. Sully turned to Emma with one eyebrow raised in consternation. "You can start the questioning there. Where is my truck?"

CHAPTER

19

BRIAR CREEK
PUBLIC LIBRARY

I 'll work it into my interview," Emma said. "Molly will be in to take your written statements, and then you can go. You should both go home and get some rest. We can talk more later."

She left and Lindsey sank into a seat at the table with her coffee and her cookie. She was so relieved that the murder investigation was over and that Sully was safe, she was sure she'd sleep for a week.

"There's one thing that makes no sense to me," Sully said.

"What's that?" Lindsey asked.

"Why me?" He took the seat beside her and sipped his coffee. He was staring out the open door into the hallway as if debating getting up and going to ask Kirk Duncan why he'd abducted him.

"What do you mean?" Lindsey asked.

"Why kidnap me?" Sully asked. "I'm not an archivist. I had nothing to do with any of it."

"Except you were on the train and you said in front of everyone in our car that you heard 'things' the night Henry was murdered. Also, when I went out into the passageway, I was wearing your coat, and we have matching pajamas," Lindsey reminded him. "Clearly, Kirk thought I was you and that you were onto him. My theory is that he kidnapped you before you could tie him to Henry's murder."

"I suppose." Sully sounded dubious.

"It all makes sense. Kirk must have hidden the Highsmith book in my bag just after we discovered Henry. Our roomette was open, and everyone was milling around in shock."

"But why?" Sully asked.

"What do you mean?"

"Why hide it in our things?" he asked.

"To keep the suspicion off himself. He had to know once Henry's body was found that the book would be evidence that he was a thief and a murderer," Lindsey speculated.

Sully shook his head. "He could have hidden it anywhere on the train. Why our bags? To have murdered a man over a book and then to just toss it aside . . . it seems off."

"Maybe he panicked," Lindsey said. "If he was the one who hid the book under my seat at the conference, then ditching the book actually is his modus operandi. Also, I'm sure he thought he'd be able to get it back. By planting it in our things, he thought he knew exactly where it was, which was why he broke into our house to retrieve it."

"He broke into our house?" Sully's eyes went wide.

"More accurately, he walked in through the back door, which wasn't locked," Lindsey said.

Sully shook his head, as if this was too much to take in. He was quiet for a moment and then said, "Perhaps Henry wasn't supposed to die, but when he did, Kirk decided to pass the book off to the person who originally found it, making them look—"

"Ah!" Lindsey gasped. "He was trying to frame me for Henry's murder!"

"Just a theory." Sully shrugged.

"No, it all makes sense. That's why he stuck the book in my bag. The plan was to stick me with the book, conveniently making me look guilty of Henry's murder, and then kidnap you to force me to trade the book for you," Lindsey said.

"There's no way Kirk did this on his own."

"Agreed." She nodded. "But who was in on it? How do we find them?"

"I think it had to be someone on the train with us," Sully said.

"Penny?" Lindsey asked.

"She makes the most sense."

"We're going back to the inn, aren't we?"

"Yup." He finished his cookie and his coffee. "I'm going to call my parents. My mom knows every cottage on the islands inside and out. If anyone can recognize it, she can."

"Okay, I'll fill out our statements." Lindsey set to work, dipping in occasionally to hear what Sully said to his parents. She watched him text the picture to them, and her phone, which he was still using, chimed with an incoming call a moment later.

"You do recognize it? It's Crater Island. Are you sure?" Sully asked. He turned to face Lindsey with his eyebrows raised. She put down her pen. Sully was listening intently and then asked, "Who is Jasmine Manwaring?

"Uh-huh," he said. "Right. Do you remember the name of the bigwig she married?" He paused to listen. And then his eyes went wide. "Bellamy? She married William Bellamy?"

Jasmine Bellamy. Lindsey blinked. Here was the tie they'd been looking for between Kirk and the cottage. His grandmother Jasmine Bellamy was Briar Creek's own Jasmine Manwaring. They had to tell Emma.

"Thanks, Mom, you are amazing," Sully said. "I have to run. See you tomorrow. Yes, we'll be careful. Love you, too."

Sully ended the call. "Did you get that?"

"Oh yeah," Lindsey said. "That explains so much. Let's go tell Emma."

They left the break room and crossed the hall to the interview room. Because Molly was in charge of the station's decorating, it wasn't exactly the plain table and hard chair of the televised crime shows. Rather, there were plants in baskets and a nice painting by a local artist of the bay, an oval table and several rolling chairs with cushions.

Emma was seated across the table from Kirk while Officer Kirkland stood inside the door.

Sully knocked on the glass wall. Emma glanced around and then huffed in annoyance.

She shook her head, but Sully wasn't put off.

"It's important," he said.

Emma shoved out of her seat and stepped out of the room, closing the door behind her. "What?"

"Kirk Duncan is the grandson of Jasmine Bellamy," he said.

"President of the Archivist Society," Lindsey added.

"And?"

"Her maiden name is Jasmine Manwaring, and she grew up on and now owns Crater Island, which my mother says is where Kirk took me. She recognized the tile flooring in the ransom picture Kirk took of me from when Jasmine had it shipped in years ago."

Emma frowned. "Does that mean Kirk grew up here?"

"I don't think so," Sully said. "He knew enough to get me out to the island, but as my mother put it, Jasmine felt she had traded up since her beginnings on the island. She wanted to sell the place, but her husband liked the idea of owning an island and wouldn't let her. As far as my mom knows, and believe me she does, none of Jasmine's children or grandchildren have ever come out to the island, as Jasmine wanted to keep her former and present lives separate."

Emma turned to face the room. "Is that all of it?"

"Yes," Sully said.

"Except," Lindsey said. Emma turned back to face them. "Except?"

"We think Kirk must have been working with someone. There's just no way he could have covered the amount of ground he did all by himself," she said.

"I was thinking the same thing," Emma said. "He's lawyered up, so I don't know if I'll be able to shake anything loose, but I'll use the grandmother angle and see. Thank you both. Now go home."

"Roger that," Sully said.

Emma pushed the door open and went inside, closing it behind her. A part of Lindsey wanted to stay and watch through the glass as Emma grilled Kirk, but she knew Emma would shoo them away. Besides, they had a stop to make.

"One problem," Sully said. "Without my truck, how are we getting to the inn?"

"Sully!" Charlie Peyton appeared in the hallway. He was dressed for the cold in a big puffy coat, hat, scarf, boots and gloves. "I'd heard they found you!" He came at Sully with his arms held wide and wrapped him in a big old bear hug.

"Good to see you, Charlie," Sully said. He hugged him in return and stepped back, giving him some room.

Charlie glanced at Lindsey. "Didn't I say he'd be all right?"

"You did," Lindsey agreed. "And I'm so grateful for all your help while Sully was missing." She turned to Sully.

"Charlie took the pets and me to the inn. In fact, he shuttled us back and forth a few times. I owe you one, actually several. I owe you several, Charlie."

She smiled at him but he just stared at her.

"Charlie, you look dead on your feet," Molly said as she entered the hallway. "You barely got any sleep last night. Shouldn't you go home and rest?"

Charlie didn't move. In fact, he didn't say a word or blink. Sully stepped back in front of him and leaned in close so that his face was only inches from Charlie's. He waved his hand in front of Charlie's open eyes.

"I think he's asleep standing up," he said.

"Let's get him to the couch in the break room, poor guy," Molly clucked.

Lindsey hurried forward, and together they took Charlie by the arms and led him to the couch in the break room. Molly followed with her hands out as if Charlie might keel over backward and she'd need to catch him. They maneuvered him to a seated position, and Lindsey took off his hat and loosened his scarf while Sully removed his boots. Together they helped him out of his coat.

"The officers crash in here a lot," Molly said. She crossed over to the cupboards and produced a pillow and blanket out of the lower one. "I'm sure no one will mind if Charlie sleeps in here, especially as it will keep him from being out on the road, which in his condition is just plain dangerous."

Lindsey lifted Charlie's head and placed it on the pillow.

"Thanks, Mom," Charlie muttered. His eyes shut and he immediately began to snore.

Sully fished Charlie's keys out of his coat pocket while Molly draped the blanket over him. "I'll move his truck for him."

Molly glanced at him and said, "I'm sure he won't mind if you use his truck to go look for yours. Of course, you'll need to leave it be and let the police check it for evidence first."

"Of course," Sully said. "I just want to find it."

"Where do you suppose your kidnapper parked it?"

"The inn," Lindsey said. "Or someplace near the inn."

"What makes you say that?" Sully asked.

"Kirk kidnapped you and got you out to one of the islands, but to make it back to the inn, he had to come back to the shore in his boat," she said. "He must have taken your keys to use your truck to get back to the inn before Emma or Kirkland noticed he was missing."

Sully nodded. "Or someone helped him kidnap me and took the keys to my truck, got back to the inn and then went to pick him up."

"Let's go," Lindsey said.

"Statements!" Molly cried.

"Of course," Lindsey said.

They finished their forms in a hurry. Lindsey wasn't worried about it because she knew they'd be doing a formal interview with Emma as soon as she had a chance.

They paused beside Charlie on their way out the door.

Lindsey reached down and put her hand on his head. "He was so worried about you."

Sully nodded. "He's like the little brother I never knew I wanted."

She smiled and put her arm through his. "Come on, let's go find your truck and Kirk's potential accomplice."

They left the police station and stopped at home to check on Heathcliff and Zelda. Lindsey made them both fried-egg sandwiches to give them fuel for their endeavor, and then they were back in Charlie's truck, searching the town. They drove right to the inn, and using it as a starting point, they worked their way out from it, scouring all of the side streets in the neighborhood. Frustratingly, there was no sign of Sully's truck.

"I'm trying not to panic," he said.

"I know," Lindsey agreed. She knew how attached he was to his beat-up old pickup truck. He'd been driving it when she first met him, and she'd become attached to it as well. It lacked all the bells and whistles, but it had one thing all of the newfangled vehicles lacked: it was as reliable as the tide. "Let's go in and see if anyone at the inn remembers seeing it."

Sully glanced at her with one eyebrow raised. "Do you think Emma would be okay with this?"

"Probably not, but this is your truck, and you deserve to find out what happened to it," she said. "And if we just happen to gather some information that indicates that Kirk had an accomplice . . . oops."

She shrugged and Sully laughed.

"Let's hope for an oops," he agreed. He drove them back to the inn and parked in the lot. The air was calm, and Lindsey was relieved not to have the polar vortex wind ripping at her coat as they trudged to the front of the building.

They stepped inside, and Michelle was at the desk. She smiled at them and said, "I heard the good news. I'm so glad you're all right, Sully."

"Me, too," he said.

"What happened?" Michelle asked. She raised her hands in a *stop* gesture. "Not that I want gory details—unless you want to share them—but truly, what happened?"

"The short version is I was approached by Kirk Duncan down on the docks, he clocked me on the head and then dumped me in his boat and carted me out to an island where I spent the duration of the storm bound and gagged until my brilliant wife managed to trade a phony book for me, giving the police the opportunity to catch Duncan."

"Wow!" Michelle said. "That's wild."

"And now we're looking for any clue to the whereabouts of Sully's truck," Lindsey said. "We figured that Kirk must have used it to come back to the inn, but we can't find it anywhere in the area, and I can't believe he ditched it to walk back to the inn in the middle of a blizzard."

"When do you think this would have happened?" Michelle asked.

Lindsey looked at Sully. "You left to take the supplies out to the island right after we got home."

"It took me a while to get the supplies together," he said. "You know how everyone is before a blizzard."

"No milk or bread," Michelle and Lindsey said together.

"Exactly," he said. "I had to drive over to the bigger grocery store on Leetes Island Road and then come back and pack up the boat. Were the supplies still there when Ian found my boat?"

"They were," Lindsey said. "Speaking of which, we need to get those supplies out to the islanders."

"No worries there," Sully said. "When I spoke to my sister, Ian was already suiting up to go."

"Good." Lindsey hated to think of the food going to waste. There was an upside to the cold. Nothing would spoil before it was delivered.

"If you want to ask around if anyone saw your truck, most of the guests are in the dining room," Michelle said. "They weren't told the specifics, but with a suspect in custody, Officer Kirkland felt it was okay to inform them they'd get to leave soon—some of them were getting downright surly—so the spirits are high."

"Good," Lindsey said. "That should make this easier."

Together, they strode toward the double doors into the dining room.

Before they could enter, Lindsey grabbed Sully. "Wait."

"What is it?" he asked.

"If Kirk was working with someone else, they believe he's trading you for the book right now," she said. "No one else knows that you were kidnapped, and I'd bet most of them don't know you were missing."

Sully nodded. "And if I walk in there, whoever was working with Kirk is going to freak out because it means Kirk failed."

"Exactly," Lindsey said. "But we can't watch all of them at once."

"No, but we can make it sound like Emma is on her way to arrest the person who was working with Kirk," Sully said.

"And whoever bolts for the exit is likely our person," Lindsey concluded. She peered around the edge of the door-frame, trying to assess how many people were in there and how many exits were viable.

Penny Minton was standing on the far side of the room by the coffee carafes. She was happily chatting with Andrew Shields, looking as if she didn't have a care in the world. Given that she was Kirk's likeliest accomplice, Lindsey found her demeanor surprising. She would have thought Penny would be anxious, wondering where Kirk was and whether or not he'd gotten the book back.

Lydia Armand was seated by herself. This, at least, seemed normal. She had a coffee in front of her, and she was scrolling through her phone with a pensive expression on her face. Lindsey saw their car attendant Patrick across the room, standing beside the only other entrance.

"There are a lot of people in there," Lindsey said. "But I only see one other way out of the room, and that's directly across from us. Somehow we have to keep an eye on the exit and the people."

"We need help, someone who's good at reading faces," Sully said. "Someone like Robbie."

"You called?" a voice asked from behind them. Lindsey yelped as Robbie popped up between them.

He grabbed Sully in a hug, picking him up in the air and forcing a laugh out of him when he set him down. "Emma told me what happened. Don't do that again, mate. You scared five years off me."

"I promise," Sully said. He stepped back and added, "No more getting knocked on the head and kidnapped."

"I don't think that's asking so much, do you?" Robbie asked Lindsey, and she shook her head.

"Not at all," she said. She frowned at Sully. "Do you think you should have a doctor examine you? Getting hit on the head is not something to ignore."

"I will," he agreed. "After we find my truck."

"Is that why you need me?" Robbie asked.

"Sort of. We *are* looking for Sully's truck," Lindsey said. "But we're also trying to determine who in that room might be Kirk Duncan's accomplice. He couldn't have kidnapped Sully on his own. We realized that whoever it is thinks Kirk made the exchange, so when Sully walks in there, they're going to make a run for it."

"And you want me to scan the faces and look for the guilty party," Robbie said.

"Yes, while keeping an eye on the doors," Sully said.

"That seems easy enough," Robbie said. "How shall we do this? I think having you stride in there is your best play, and I'll make an announcement about your truck. That will give the accomplice time to try and escape. Yes?"

"I can't think of anything better," Lindsey said.

"Me neither," Sully agreed.

"Okay, then, follow my lead," Robbie said. He strode into the room and hopped up onto the seat of a nearby chair. "Attention! Attention, please." It took a moment for the room to grow quiet, but since it was Robbie Vine, the conversations stopped as everyone turned to see what the famous actor had to say. "We're wondering if anyone saw a beat-up old pickup truck like something an old-timey farmer would drive—"

"Hey!" Sully protested, but Robbie continued on. Lindsey scanned the faces of the people in the room, trying to determine whether anyone looked scared or startled by Sully's sudden appearance.

"It would have been sometime yesterday, probably late afternoon or early evening, possibly later?"

There were some murmurs and some mutters, and people shook their heads or shrugged, but no one acknowledged seeing such a truck. Lindsey didn't see anyone making a run for the door, but several people were up and moving toward the coffee and muffins on the far side of the room.

"Well, it was worth a shot," Robbie said as he climbed down.

"Wait!" Penny cried. She had one hand up as if she were signaling a waiter. Everyone in the room turned to face her, and she said, "Didn't I see you getting into an old beater of a truck last night, Lydia?"

The entire room swiveled their attention to Lydia, who had risen from her seat and was walking across the room. She was carrying her coffee cup but was headed toward the far exit, not the carafes. She stopped and glanced over her shoulder at Penny and said, "Ha! That's rich!"

CHAPTER

20

BRIAR CREEK
PUBLIC LIBRARY

Lindsey felt the hair on the back of her neck prickle. She'd heard those exact words before, but where? She tried to picture the person saying them, but she couldn't get the mental picture into focus.

"What a delightful little imagination you have, Penny. I can assure you, I have never set foot in a pickup truck of any kind ever."

Dressed in a tailored navy suit with a pin-striped silk blouse and stiletto heels, it was hard to picture her climbing into a pickup truck. Except . . . the memory snapped into place.

"You were the person in the stairwell," Lindsey said. She pointed at Lydia. "Not Penny."

"Excuse me?" Lydia slowly turned to face Lindsey. She

had one eyebrow raised higher than the other as if offended by Lindsey's impertinence.

"Last night, I overheard Kirk talking to a woman in the stairwell. I assumed it was Penny because he'd been chasing her for days, but it wasn't. It was you."

Lydia scoffed. "You're delusional."

"Am I?" Lindsey asked. "Robbie was with me when Kirk came out of the stairwell, wearing his coat, boots, hat and scarf. Where had he been that he needed to be so bundled up?"

Lydia was breathing through her nose, nostrils flaring. "I'm sure I have no idea. I was in my room all evening."

"Really? Are you sure you don't want to get ahead of this and tell us what really happened, Lydia?" Lindsey asked. "I'm quite certain with a murder charge hanging over him, Kirk will tell all."

Lydia's jaw tightened. "I'm sure whatever happens to Kirk Duncan has nothing to do with me."

"Doesn't it though?" Lindsey asked. She decided to bluff with the information Kirk had given them when they'd caught him trying to swap Sully for the book. She'd been turning over what Kirk had said in her mind, and this was the only angle that made sense. "Jasmine made a mistake with the donation for the silent auction, didn't she? She was the anonymous donor of the Highsmith book, but she didn't mean to donate that particular item, and you and Kirk had to get it back. How am I doing?"

"I don't know. Are you pitching this as a fictional novel?

It's quite boring, I'd say," Lydia protested, but two bright spots of color bloomed on her cheeks.

Lindsey started to pace the room. She looked at Robbie and said, "Call Emma." And then at Sully and said, "Block the far door, please."

"You can't keep me here." Lydia began to charge toward the main entrance.

Penny shot in front of her and ordered, "Stop."

Her tone brooked no refusal. She looked at Lindsey and said, "Go on."

"You murdered Henry over the book, didn't you?" Lindsey asked Lydia.

"Um, no." Lydia's voice dripped with sarcasm. "In case you missed it, Kirk Duncan is in custody for that, which is why the rest of us have been told we're free to go as soon as we can get transportation out of this backwater."

"How did you know he was in custody when that information hasn't been made public?" Lindsey asked. "Could it be because you know that Kirk was holding Sully in exchange for the book, and if Sully is here, well, then it's obvious Kirk failed?"

"I have no idea what you're talking about," Lydia said. "I simply overheard someone say something about Kirk being at the police station. That's all. Not a big deal."

"No you didn't, because no one knew. And I'd say letting him take the fall for you is probably going to be a pretty big deal for him, don't you think?" Lindsey asked.

"I don't think his grandmother Jasmine Bellamy is going to appreciate it either."

"Are you finished with your fantasy story?" Lydia cried. She tossed her phone into her bag. "I've heard enough. I'm leaving."

"Will you be taking Sully's truck?" Lindsey asked. "If not, perhaps you could tell us where you parked it."

"Again, I have no clue what you're referring to," Lydia said.

"I do!" Penny raised her hand and crossed the room to join them. "You see, I happen to know that you're actually working for Jasmine Bellamy, who has an ongoing feud with Mr. Barclay."

"Mr. Barclay is my employer." Lydia straightened up. The look on her face was fierce. "I represent his interests, certainly not those of his rival."

"I expect that was true until Jasmine introduced you to her grandson," Penny said. She leaned back on her heels and added, "You see, I work for Mr. Barclay, too."

Lydia gave her a side-eye. "No, you worked for Henry Standish."

"Did I?" Penny asked. She took off her glasses and pulled her hair out of its tight bun. Her hair fell down around her shoulders in a cascade of nut brown. "Honey, come and explain things to Ms. Armand, won't you?"

She looked over her shoulder at Andrew, and he strode forward, stopping beside her and placing his hand on her lower back in a show of support.

"My wife works with me," he said. "Penny is actually

Penny Shields, and she's a licensed private investigator, and together we own Shields Investigations and are currently employed by Holden Barclay."

"What?" Lydia cried. She glanced between them, looking confused and angry. "How? Why? What could you possibly be doing for Mr. Barclay?"

"Mr. Barclay has always felt unsettled about the items that went missing during Henry Standish's time as his curator. Several months ago, he hired us to find the materials to prove once and for all what happened," Penny said. "We had no luck until one of the titles appeared in the catalog for the silent auction at the conference. Imagine our surprise. That's why Henry handed it to me at the conference. He knew I was working for Barclay as an investigator, as Mr. Barclay had told him he was tracking the missing items. Henry thought it was his chance to prove his innocence once and for all. When you handed him the book, Lindsey, he recognized it immediately."

"He certainly didn't show it at the time," Sully said. "He looked mostly annoyed."

"I know," Penny agreed. "But trust me when I tell you he was very much relieved that the book had been found. We both were. He told the conference goers that the book had been withdrawn by the donor, so that bidders wouldn't panic about a thief having access to the items. Henry knew his reputation rested on having possession of that book, so he played his part and gave nothing away. Much like me with Kirk, pretending to be interested in him was definitely the hardest part of this job." She shuddered.

"But Henry was so mean to you at the conference and on the train," Lindsey said. "That was an act?"

Penny nodded. "We thought it was the best strategy to maintain my cover. Henry didn't want to appear deferential to me in any way. We agreed to let everyone wonder where the item had gone after Henry gave it to me at the conference, but I turned it over to Henry that evening. He was looking forward to calling Mr. Barclay and letting him know it had been found. He chose to wait until he could verify who the anonymous donor was. Sadly, he never got the chance to do that or make the call."

"Henry lost all of the records. There's no way you can prove that the Highsmith book was one of the titles that went missing," Lydia said.

"Oh, but we can," Penny said.

"Because it came from Jasmine Bellamy," Lindsey said. "She was the anonymous donor."

Penny looked at her with approval. "Very good deduction."

"Not really," Lindsey said. "Kirk admitted as much." She glanced at Lydia and saw her mouth form a tight line.

"Andrew was able to determine that the item was donated from the Bellamy collection. Unfortunately, he discovered it after Henry was murdered," Penny said.

"You can't seriously think I had anything to do with any of that," Lydia said. "I work for Mr. Barclay. I am loyal to him."

"Are you?" Penny asked. "It seems to me that you're

angling for the position of granddaughter-in-law to Jasmine Bellamy, which carries much more prestige, don't you agree?"

Lindsey gasped. Now it was all making sense.

"I don't mean to be thick, as Robbie would say, but I've lost the thread. What are we talking about?" Sully asked. "And where's my truck?"

"Lydia is involved with Kirk, who is Jasmine Bellamy's grandson," Lindsey explained. "She was also installed as Barclay's curator by Mrs. Bellamy, which means that Lydia is actually spying on her boss Mr. Barclay for Mrs. Bellamy because there's bad blood there."

"This is ridiculous," Lydia said. "You can't prove any of this."

"Actually, I think I can," Lindsey said.

Penny looked at her with interest.

Lindsey decided to go with a big bluff. "The volume of *Strangers on a Train* that you stole from Holden Barclay is identifiable because of the initials H.B. that Mr. Barclay scribbled onto the endpapers, a notorious habit of his. You knew if anyone saw it and if it was discovered that Jasmine was the anonymous donor, then they would figure out it had to be you stealing items from Holden Barclay for Jasmine Bellamy, which would of course call into question your original audit of Barclay's collection and the fact that you got Henry Standish's job. So you and your lover Kirk Duncan decided to steal the book back from the auction so that your relationship with the Bellamys wasn't exposed."

"Everyone knows that Barclay does that with his initials. Someone could easily put those initials in the book to frame me. It signifies nothing," Lydia said.

"Except Kirk admitted that his grandmother donated the Highsmith book to the auction by mistake, and I bet it has those initials in it. You're the only person who has access to the collection other than Barclay himself," Lindsey said. "It had to be you, and given that Henry recognized it as one of the missing items from the audit, well, it really wasn't looking good for you, was it?"

Lydia swallowed. She stared at Lindsey, looking as though she'd like to strangle her. It was definitely intimidating, but when Lindsey thought about what Lydia and Kirk had done to Sully, she found she simply didn't care.

"I suspect Kirk pulled the book from the auction, which should have resolved the matter, but something went wrong and it landed under my seat at the conference. What happened? Did Kirk panic? Lose it? Was it stolen? Feel free to enlighten us."

Lydia stared unblinking.

"No matter," Lindsey said. "I'm sure Kirk will be happy to fill in the gaps when he realizes you'd let him take the entire rap for the murder."

"According to you, Kirk is in police custody, and it would appear that he murdered Henry. Why are you trying to pull me into this?" Lydia protested.

"Occam's razor," Robbie muttered. Lindsey sent him a look and he shrugged. "I'm just saying."

"I don't need to pull you into this, Lydia," Lindsey said.

"You inserted yourself the moment you approached Henry on the train and demanded the book back. When he refused to give you the book unless you admitted that he was set up by you in your bogus audit, you had no choice but to kill him. A confession like that would destroy your career, you'd be of no use to Mrs. Bellamy. You'd lose your position, and most likely your relationship with Kirk. So you fought over the book, and Henry fell? Tripped? What?"

Lydia's eyes darted from side to side as if looking for an escape. There was none. Every single person in the room was watching her.

"After Henry died," Lindsey continued, "you fled his compartment, dressed all in black. It was you that I saw in the passageway that night."

Lydia shook her head. She rolled her eyes. "This has gone past the point of ridiculous. I'm leaving."

Emma stepped into the doorway beside Sully, and together they blocked the exit. She crossed her arms over her chest. "Not yet I think, Ms. Armand. I missed the beginning, but I believe we were just getting to the good part."

"To sum up," Robbie said. "Lydia murdered Henry. Apparently, the book that you have in the police vault was stolen from Henry's former employer Holden Barclay and given to this Jasmine Bellamy, whose grandson you have in custody, who is also apparently involved with Ms. Armand, who has been stealing books from Barclay to give to Bellamy. When one accidentally ended up in the silent auction, Lydia had to get it back to save her reputation and Jasmine Bellamy's because the item in question was one of the books that Henry Standish couldn't account for in the audit that cost him his job." Robbie paused to take a breath. "Lydia and Henry fought over the book on the train, and he died. Not sure if it was premeditated, but that's up to the prosecutors, yeah?"

"Yeah." Emma nodded. She scanned the room, taking in all of the faces before she turned to Sully. "We found your truck."

"Really?" He perked up and then looked wary. "Is it all right?"

"Perfectly fine," Emma said. "Which is a lucky thing, because it was buried in a snowdrift, and a plow was about to have a go at it until he saw one of the taillights sticking out."

Sully put his hand over his heart and squeezed his chest. "That's good news."

Emma nodded. "They towed it out, and it's parked out front. We did have to jimmy the locked door to check out the interior."

"I have backup keys, you could have just asked," Sully said.

"Sorry," Emma said. "But we did retrieve a burner phone from the console, and guess what we found in the camera roll?"

"Pictures of Sully?" Lindsey asked.

"And texts to you and another unidentified number," Emma said. She held her hand out to Lydia. "Your bag."

Lydia clutched it to her chest. "No. You need a warrant or something."

"Do I?" Emma asked. "Probable cause." She snatched the bag out of Lydia's arms and opened it. She peered inside and then pulled a blue latex glove from her pocket and began to sift through Lydia's belongings. In moments, she had gathered two phones. She pressed the buttons on the generic one.

"And the phone number called from the burner phone matches this one," she said. She glanced over her shoulder at Officer Kirkland. "Take her in for questioning. I'll be right behind you."

"You can't prove anything," Lydia spat. "Someone planted that phone in my bag. I've never seen it before in my life."

Officer Kirkland began reciting her rights while securing her hands behind her back.

"I'll sue you," Lydia cried. "I'll make sure you lose your job, and the best you can do is be a security guard in a mall."

Emma made a shooing motion with her hands. Kirkland hauled Lydia out of the room, and Officer Wilcox, who'd been outside the door, fell into step behind him. The echoes of Lydia's fury reverberated down the hallway, and no one spoke until she was fully gone.

"Are my truck keys in there?" Sully asked.

Emma opened the bag. "Yup. But now they're evidence, and so is your truck."

Sully ran a hand over his face. Lindsey moved to stand beside him and put her arm around his waist. He looked as exhausted as she felt.

"Emma will take good care of her," she said. "Don't worry."

"I promise," Emma said. "Besides, no one is leaving the inn until we take the statement of everyone who overheard what just happened in this room, and by then my officer should be done fingerprinting and photographing the truck."

Sully stood there without blinking, just staring at her. "Sully?" Emma waved a hand in front of his face.

"I think he just fell asleep standing up," Lindsey said.

Emma's lips twitched. "If I tell him he can go catch a catnap in your old room down the hall, will he wake up?"

"No, but I bet I can get him there," Lindsey said. "Come on, Husband, a power nap awaits."

Sully groaned, but he threw an arm over her shoulders, and together they walked down the hallway to her former room. The door was open, and they collapsed onto the bed. Sully was unconscious before his head landed on the pillow, but Lindsey blinked at the ceiling.

Occam's razor indeed. She was never going to hear the end of it from Robbie that Lydia, who had been the most logical murder suspect, had in fact proved to be the murderer. Darn it.

T his was a wild ride," Violet said. She held up her copy of *Strangers on a Train*. "Highsmith can turn up the tension like nobody."

"I know," Paula agreed. "But you can't really feel sympathy for the characters because if they weren't terrible, too, they wouldn't get embroiled in the bad guy's schemes."

Paula was seated at the end of the table with this week's craft beside her. She had decided they needed to make a to-be-read jar. While discussing *Strangers on a Train*, they'd written ideas for titles to read for their upcoming meetings on colorful scraps of paper that they then put in the jar. Paula had labeled it the TBR jar, and they would draw their next title from it at the end of the meeting.

"So, Highsmith created the original unlikable protagonists?" Mayor Cole asked. She had come over from her office at the town hall to join them.

"Completely, it's glorious," Charlene agreed. She had insisted on coming to this week's meeting, as she loved Highsmith's thrillers and others, like the ones written by Rachel Howzell Hall. Lindsey assumed it was the newsperson in her.

They were seated at the table in the crafternoon room with a large chicken potpie, a loaf of hot buttered bread, a garden salad and a pot of cinnamon tea. While the blizzard was gone and the town had dug out, New England was having a polar-vortex-driven cold snap where the temperature read ten degrees below zero but felt like thirty below. Lindsey had been in charge of the food this week, and she had decided they needed to carbo-load to fight off the chilly temps.

"Speaking of unlikable, what's the update on Lydia Armand and Kirk Duncan?" Nancy asked.

"Oh, wait for me," Beth cried as she hurried into the

room. She was dressed as a big old bumblebee, and Lindsey suspected she had chosen bees as the theme for story time because she was longing for spring.

Beth unzipped her extra-large yellow hooded sweatshirt, upon which she had sewn thick black stripes and wings on the body and antennae on the hood. She shrugged out of it, dropping the pillows she'd stuffed it with onto the floor. She adjusted her cable knit tunic sweater over leggings and said, "That's better. What did I miss?"

"We were just pivoting from discussing *Strangers on a Train* to Lydia Armand and Kirk Duncan," Nancy said. She was dishing a plate for Beth and set it down at the empty seat.

"What is happening with them?" Beth asked.

"After what they did to my brother, I hope they're getting exactly what they deserve," Mary said. She stabbed a cherry tomato in her salad like it was an enemy's eye. "Not to mention that poor Henry Standish."

Lindsey agreed with her. They had a lot to answer for, which, according to Emma, there would be. The case had gathered more and more evidence, and it appeared even the affluent and powerful Jasmine Bellamy wouldn't be able to save them. Not that she had tried. According to her attorney, the two of them had operated without her knowledge or consent. Yeah, right.

"Lydia has been charged with the murder of Henry Standish," Lindsey said. "After he discovered she was planning to flee town and let him take the fall for all of it, Kirk had a change of heart and confessed all to Emma. He stole the book from the silent auction, forcing them to update the program in the final hours. He was supposed to pass it off to Lydia at the conference, but he panicked, thinking security was onto him, and hid it under my seat during the Wainwright lecture."

"Not skilled in the criminal arts, is he?" Nancy asked.

"No. Anyway, he said Lydia was the one who fought with Henry. She surprised Henry when he was entering his roomette after a trip to the restroom. They fought over the book, which was in his suitcase on the upper bunk. Henry fell, breaking his neck, and she took the book and ran. She was the person I saw in the hallway who was dressed all in black."

"I thought that was Kirk when he kidnapped Sully," Beth said.

"He wore the same outfit," Lindsey said. "He said it was Lydia's idea, and I suspect she was trying to frame him at that point. He'll be tried as an accomplice in the murder, and he'll have to answer for kidnapping Sully, so it's not looking rosy for him either, but the murder charge is all Lydia's."

"Robbie said the entire case was a perfect example of Occam's razor," Violet said. She glanced at Lindsey, who rolled her eyes.

"He got lucky, declaring it was Lydia early on," she said. "He's going to crow about that forever, isn't he?"

"Yes." Violet laughed and the others joined in.

Lindsey grinned. She supposed it was a small sacrifice for everything to have turned out all right. Sully was home.

Holden Barclay was going to get his books back. And Henry's murderer had been caught and his reputation restored.

A plaque was being crafted in his honor to hang in the office of the archivist conference headquarters. From now on, when archivists talked about Henry Standish, it would be about his accomplishments instead of his scandal. Lindsey supposed it was too little too late, but she liked to think that somehow Henry knew that justice had been served, and his legacy preserved.

In the end, wasn't that all anyone could hope for? To know that they made a difference and to be remembered well.

# Crafternoon Guide

What is a crafternoon? Simply put, it's where friends gather to discuss a book they've read while they share food and do a craft. Here are some ideas to get you started.

# Readers Guide for
## *Strangers on a Train*

*by Patricia Highsmith*

1. Much of *Fatal First Edition* centers on a book that was the basis for a movie. Which do you prefer, books or their movie adaptations? Can you think of any movies that were better than the book? Which ones and why?

2. The premise of the book is that two strangers swap murders. Does this seem like it would work? Why or why not?

3. There is not much to like about Highsmith's protagonist Guy Haines, even though he is pulled into a situation not of his own making. How did you feel about his character? Do you think he could have made better choices and changed the outcome?

4. What is the assumption that Guy makes about the stranger (Bruno) whom he meets on the train? How does Bruno prove him wrong?

5. Bruno forces himself into Guy's life, making it impossible for him to ignore him. Have you ever dealt with anyone like this in your life? How did you deal with them?

6. Guy and Bruno meet on a train. What do you think is the significance of this? What does the train symbolize?

7. The novel insinuates that any person can commit murder. Do you agree or disagree?

# Craft
## A TBR Jar

**A TBR (to be read) jar is an excellent way to work through your own to-be-read pile or to use as a way to recommend titles to other readers.**

*A clean, clear jar with a wide enough opening to fit your
    hand into and a lid
Plain or colored paper
Scissors
Markers*

Cut the paper into rectangles or squares or whatever shape you like. Write down one title from your TBR pile onto each slip of paper. Fold the papers and put them in the jar. Put the lid on. When you need to choose a title to read but can't decide, simply select a slip of paper from the jar, and that's your next book. If you want to get really fancy, you can fold the slips of paper into origami 3D stars.

# Recipes

## BARBECUE PORK SLIDERS WITH COLESLAW

1 pork roast (4 to 6 pounds), boneless
⅓ cup pork rub
2 tablespoons apple cider vinegar
1 cup barbecue sauce

For the sliders:

24 slider buns
1 red onion, thinly sliced
1 jar dill pickle chips
2 cups deli coleslaw

Rub the pork roast with the pork rub. Place in a slow cooker (Crockpot). Add apple cider vinegar and cook on low heat for 8 hours. Once the pork is tender, use two forks to shred the meat.

Add the barbecue sauce, stirring to evenly coat the meat. To assemble the sliders, place shredded pork on a bun, and top with pickles, red onion and coleslaw. Serve while the meat is still warm.

## COWBOY COOKIES

*2 cups rolled oats*
*2 cups all-purpose flour*
*½ teaspoon baking powder*
*¾ teaspoon baking soda*
*½ teaspoon salt*
*¼ teaspoon cinnamon*
*1 cup unsalted butter, softened*
*1 cup brown sugar, lightly packed*
*⅔ cup granulated sugar*
*2 large eggs, room temperature*
*1 teaspoon vanilla*
*2 cups semisweet chocolate chips*
*1 cup chopped pecans*
*1 cup flaked sweetened coconut*
*Flaky salt to garnish, optional*

Preheat oven to 350°F. Line a cookie sheet with parchment paper. In a medium bowl, whisk together the oats, flour, baking powder, baking soda, salt and cinnamon, and set aside. In a large bowl, cream together the butter, sugars, eggs and vanilla. Mix in the dry ingredients until well incorporated. Stir in the chocolate chips, pecans and coconut. Using a tablespoon, drop scoops of dough onto the cookie sheet, leaving 2 to 3 inches between cookies. Bake 12 to 14 minutes, until golden brown. Remove them from the oven and sprinkle with flaky salt, if desired. Makes approximately 4 dozen.

# Acknowledgments

First, I have to thank my longtime friend Kate Carlisle. She let me take her Bibliophile Mystery characters, Brooklyn Wainwright and Derek Stone, and invite them to play. Yes, I did have her read the first chapter and give her approval, because I didn't want her to think I was going to murder them off. LOL. I am very fortunate to have both Kate and our fellow plot group buddy Paige Shelton in my life to offer encouragement, ideas and shenanigans when required. Special shout-out to our other plot group pal Hannah Dennison, who resides in England but pops in when she can.

As always, I am so grateful for my team Kate Seaver, Amanda Maurer and Christina Hogrebe. They keep me on task, and offer their wisdom and advice, making my finished work so much better than the proposals I turn into them. Much thanks to Jessica Mangicaro, Dache' Rogers, Kaila

Mundell-Hill, Kim-Salina I, and Stacy Edwards. And, as always, I am so grateful for my cover artist, Julie Greene, and the art department for giving this series the most brilliant covers.

On a personal note, I am ever thankful for my family and friends, who tolerate my weird working hours and frequent distraction. Special nod to my assistant, Christie Conlee, who takes on the heavy lifting of reader outreach, promotion, ad and swag design and social media maintenance whenever I need her. I am so very fortunate to have so many wonderful people on this creative journey.

Keep reading for an excerpt from
Jenn McKinlay's next novel . . .

# LOVE AT FIRST BOOK

E m, are you all right?" Samantha Gale, my very best friend in the entire world, answered her phone on the fourth ring. Her voice was rough with sleep, and it belatedly occurred to me that nine o'clock in the morning in Finn's Hollow, Ireland, was four o'clock in the morning in Oak Bluffs, Martha's Vineyard.

"Oh, I'm sorry. Damn it, I woke you up, didn't I?" I asked, knowing full well by then that I had and feeling awful about it.

"No, it's fine," Sam said. "I told you when you left that I'm always here for you." There was a low grumbling in the background and she added, "And Ben says he's here for you, too."

That made me laugh. Sam and Ben had become couple

goals for me. Not that I thought I'd ever find anything like the connection they'd made, but they kept the pilot light of my innermost hope aflame.

"Thank you and thank Ben," I said. "I'm going to hang up now and let you go back to sleep. Forget I ever called."

"Emily Allen, don't you dare hang up on me," Sam said. Now she sounded fully awake. *Oops.*

"No, really I—" I began, but she interrupted me.

"Tell me why you're calling, otherwise I'll worry, and no one wants that." There was more grumbling in the background. Sam laughed and said, "Ben says he's begging you to tell me so that I don't drive him crazy with speculation."

I grinned. She would, too. Then I grew serious.

Glancing around the Last Chapter, the quaint bookshop in which I was presently standing, I noted objectively that it was a book lover's dream come true. A three-story stone building chock-full of books of all kinds with a small café at the back of the first floor, where the scent of fresh-brewed coffee, berry-filled scones and cinnamon pastry permeated the air. I felt myself lean in that direction as if the delicious aromas were reeling me in.

One of the shop employees had unlocked the front door of the shop a few moments ago, and I had drifted in behind a handful of customers who'd been waiting. I'd been agog ever since.

This was it. The bookshop where I'd be working for the next year. My heart was pounding and my palms were sweaty. The black wool turtleneck sweater I was wearing, in an attempt to defeat the early November chill, felt as if it were choking me, and I was quite sure the pain spearing across my head meant I was having an aneurysm.

"I'm supposed to meet my boss in a few minutes, and I think I'm having a heart attack or potentially a stroke," I said.

There was a beat of silence on the other end of the phone. Then Sam said, "Tell me your symptoms."

I listed them all, and she noted each one with an *uh-huh*, which told me nothing whatsoever as to what she was thinking about my condition. I was three thousand miles away and starting a new job in a bookshop, having put my career as a librarian on Martha's Vineyard on hold to chase some crazy fantasy where I traveled to a foreign destination and lived a life full of adventure.

"I think I'm going to throw up," I groaned.

"Take a deep breath," Sam said. "You know the drill— in for eight seconds, hold for four, out for eight."

I sucked in a breath. My head pounded. "I can't. It makes my head throb. See? Aneurysm."

"Or a lack-of-caffeine headache," she said. "Have you had any coffee yet?"

Come to think of it, I had not. I'd been too nervous to make any before I left my cottage this morning, so the potential for this skull splitter to be from coffee deprivation seemed likely.

"No," I said. "And I see where you're going, but I still have brutal nausea and I'm sweating. I bet I have a fever. Maybe it's food poisoning from the airplane food last night. I did have the beef Stroganoff."

"You ate airplane food?" Sam sounded as incredulous as if I'd confessed I ate ice cream off the bathroom floor. She was a professional chef, so not a big surprise.

"I know, I know," I said. "It's pure preservatives. I'll likely be dead within the hour."

There was a lengthy pause where I imagined Sam was practicing her last words to me, wanting to get them just right.

"Em, you know I love you like a sister, right?" she asked.

Hmm. This did not sound like the beginning of a vow of friendship into the afterlife.

"I do," I said. "I also know that's how you would start a sentence that I'm not going to like."

"You're panicking, Em," Sam said. Her voice was full of empathy and patience. "And you and I both know that the bout of hypochondria you dealt with last summer was how you coped with your anxiety and your unhappiness."

"But I'm not unhappy," I protested. "I'm living the dream, thousands of miles away from everyone I've ever known and loved, in a quaint village in County Kerry where the green is the greenest green I've ever seen and there's a sheep staring at me over the top of every stone wall. Seriously, I'm drowning in charm, which is probably why I'm about to keel over dead."

A sound came from my phone that sounded like someone stepping on a duck.

"Are you laughing at me?" I asked. Rude but understandable.

"No, never," Sam said. She cleared her throat. "I just

think you might be freaking out a little because it's your first day of work at your new job."

"I'm not," I protested. I was. I absolutely was. "I just think I need to get on the train back to Dublin and hop on the next flight home before they discover I have some highly contagious pox or plague and I'm quarantined to a thatched stone cottage to live out my days in a fairy-infested forest, talking to the trees and hedgehogs while farming potatoes."

"Have you ever considered that you read too much?" Sam asked.

"No!" I cried, and I heard Ben, also a librarian and formerly my boss, protest as well.

Sam laughed. She did like to goad us.

"Just think, if I leave now, we can meet for coffee and pastries at the Grape tomorrow morning. Doesn't that sound nice?" I asked.

"While I'd love to see you, you know that, you have to stay in Ireland and see your journey through," Sam said. "Besides, if you go home now, your mother will guilt you into never leaving again, not to mention clobber you with the dreaded 'I told you so.'"

"Fair point." I sighed. I pulled away to glance at the display on my phone. My mother had already called five times and texted twelve, and I hadn't even been in Ireland for twenty-four hours yet. I tabled that problem to deal with the one at hand. "I still think I might pass out, and then I'll likely lose the job and this entire conversation becomes moot."

"You're not going to pass out," Sam said. "Find a place to sit down. Can you do that?"

"I think so." I was standing in the stacks—okay, more accurately, hiding in the fiction section. The shelves were dark wood, long and tall and stuffed with books. They comforted me. Scattered randomly amid the shelving units were step stools. I found one and sat down.

"Are you sitting?" Sam asked.

"Yes."

"Good, now put your head between your knees," she ordered.

"Um." I was wearing a formfitting gray wool pencil skirt. I tried to maneuver my head down. No luck. The skirt was too snug. The closest I could get was to look over my knees at my very cute black ankle boots. "Sorry, Sam, nothing is getting between these knees. Not even a hot Irishman."

Sam chuckled, but over that I heard a strangled noise behind me, and I straightened up and turned around to see a man in jeans and an Aran sweater, holding his fist to his mouth, looking as if he were choking. He had thick, wavy black hair, and blue eyes so dark they were almost the same shade as his hair. Also, if I wasn't mistaken, judging by the picture I'd seen on the Last Chapter's website, he was my new boss.